T0109786

A LONG WALK FROM GAZA

A LONG WALK FROM GAZA

A NOVEL BY
ASMAA ALATAWNA

TRANSLATED BY

CALINE NASRALLAH & MICHELLE HARTMAN

Interlink Books

An imprint of Interlink Publishing Group, Inc.
Northampton, Massachusetts

First published in 2024 by

Interlink Books
An imprint of Interlink Publishing Group, Inc.
46 Crosby Street, Northampton, MA 01060
www.interlinkbooks.com

Text copyright © Asmaa Alatawna, 2019, 2024
English traslation copyright © Michelle Hartman and
Caline Nasrallah, 2024

Originally published in Arabic as *Sura Mafquda* (صورة مفقودة)
by Dar al Saqi, Beirut, Lebanon, 2019

All rights reserved; no part of this publication may be reproduced,
stored in a retrieval system, or transmitted, in any form or by
any means, electronic, mechanical, photocopying, recording or
otherwise, without the prior written permission of the publisher.

Library of Congress Cataloging-in-Publication data available
ISBN-13: 978-1-62371-685-1

Cover art features images by Spencer Scott Pugh and
Resul Mentes on Unsplash

Printed and bound in the United States of America

CONTENTS

PART ONE
LEAVE

I

A body on the cobblestones. Just lying there. I shake him gently to see if he is still alive. Nothing. I press my ear to his chest to check for a heartbeat. My eyes dart around on the off chance someone is passing by so late at night. But there is only deathly silence. Just water trickling from the mouth of a stone lion into the fountain at the center of Place Saint-Étienne, facing the church, in Toulouse. My first instinct is to splash his face with this cold water. I cup my hands under the lion's mouth. The cold water brings him to. A cough struggles its way out of his throat. He is still alive, breathing. I drag him to the edge of the fountain and prop him upright to make it easier to get water into his mouth. He smells rank, of vomit and urine. His breath is laced with alcohol. Every time he moves, I catch a stronger, fresher whiff of him. It's the same stench of the dead rats Abu Riyala used to hunt in the alleys back home in Gaza.

Vomit dots his coat and fingerless wool gloves. I rinse my hands in the cold fountain water and check my watch. It's nearly four in the morning. I make sure he's OK one last time, and my eyes drift back to the lion. Somehow they look eerily alike. Water spills from its mouth almost like vomit. I race off so I don't miss my appointment. Nathalie is already there. She's waiting for me outside the Toulouse Prefecture building, leaning against a small car. She hands me a hot coffee; I use it to warm up my freezing fingers, pulling up the hood of my long winter coat to cover my damp hair.

Nathalie is forty something. She's slight, with cropped black hair. Time has left traces on her face. She's spent so much time buried in paperwork that she has to wear thick prescription glasses, like al-Bilbeisi, the man who owned the only shop in my neighborhood in Gaza. I've never seen her with makeup on, or in a dress or skirt. Not once. I assume this is because she works on matters of life and death—she's a lawyer, she argues immigration and refugee claims in court.

Judges probably wouldn't see her the same way if she stood up in court to defend refugees wearing clothes that attract attention. I know from experience that I have to wear neutral tones and downplay my femininity if I want to be taken seriously. If I show up wearing lipstick and a pretty dress, how could I possibly claim to be a penniless refugee fleeing certain death? My thoughts wander off. But Nathalie's voice brings me right back to where I am—in front of the red automated security gate, its black surveillance cameras monitoring the movement of our bodies in the darkness.

As the crowd slowly swells, we move closer. My cheek is flat against the cold metal of the gate, and I press my hand to it to secure my spot at the front of the long queue. Nathalie disappears into the chaotic throng of bodies that somehow move as one. It's like a school of fish that swoops first right and then left, all together, feeding on plankton. At 9 AM sharp the automatic gate creaks open. We all immediately start climbing over each other in a struggle to reach the front before the ticket window closes.

We make it into the modern-looking building to be greeted by a circular kiosk concealing the reception sitting inside. We see only excessively long red fingernails pointing the way to the area for new asylum seekers. We dutifully queue up between two imaginary lines. We focus hard on staying within them. Otherwise we'll get yelled at by the security guard. She walks up and down, monitoring our every move, waiting to ambush us, just like Miss Zainab used to when we were children at the Dalal al-Mughrabi School for Refugees. We are different races and different colors but have all come here for the same reason. We all have the same basic desire. To stay alive.

Nathalie lets out a loud sigh. Tense and fidgeting nervously, she tells me in English that she is ashamed of the humiliating treatment we have to endure every morning. She's loud enough for the security guard to hear across the room. She keeps talking and telling me that she and some other pro bono lawyers from

Amnesty International have made an official request to the Director of the Prefecture to get chairs for the waiting room—at least enough for pregnant women, children, and the elderly. On and on she keeps talking.

Secretly, I pray that the security guard can't understand her. I'm afraid she'll take her revenge out on me, block my request, and send me back to where I came from. I want to assure Nathalie that I don't feel insulted or disrespected. Waking up at three o'clock every morning, coming here, and waiting for the iron gate to swing open is nowhere nearly as humiliating as what I've endured at the border crossings controlled by the Israeli occupation army. It can't compare to the humiliation and emotional turmoil I experienced at the hands of my father, my family, my whole neighborhood back in Gaza. I wish she'd just be quiet, even just for a bit. I need the morning to go smoothly so I can get the document that will keep me from having to go back to point zero. To inevitable death. Because even if my body doesn't die, my spirit will. The people in my neighborhood will make sure of it.

It's finally my turn. Nathalie speaks to the person in charge about my case for a long time, in French. The only word I understand is *Palestine*. It sounds almost the same in French and English. He staples my passport picture to a paper, stamps it, and hands it to her. I can still see the ink touch the paper, still hear the stamp seal itself against it. Nathalie then hands it on to me. She explains that the three empty squares must be stamped before the end of each month, by a specific date. I have to do this until a final decision is made to grant me a residence card to legitimize and legalize my stay in France.

Three months come and go. Then another three. I wake up before dawn. I arrive at the gate by four in the morning. I make my way through the crowd to get my square stamped. I do this for two years.

II

I arrived in Madrid in the summer of 2001. José had finally helped me get out of Gaza, out of the prison I was living in. He was a Spanish teacher I'd met through my work at a Spanish news agency. He'd worked on archaeological digs and followed his Jewish girlfriend to Palestine, where she was excavating a site in Jerusalem. He'd decided to live with her so they could work together, digging in occupied Palestine. They were hunting for antiquities in Jerusalem when I couldn't even go there. When they broke up, José decided to look for work as a Spanish teacher. Al-Azhar University had opened in the nineties, so he stayed in Gaza instead of heading back to Spain.

I realized then that him breaking up with his Jewish girlfriend and coming to Gaza may have been my salvation. The Institut français had refused to support my application for a visa to France. Rather than wallow in disappointment, I decided to get close to José and ask him to help me get a visa to Spain instead. I knew this would annoy a friend of mine at university whom I'd noticed was trying to get close to him too, but it didn't matter. I thought long and hard about my circumstances and everything happening around me. I could tell that José was getting increasingly attached to me, and this weighed heavily on my conscience. But I ultimately found a way to ease my guilt. I got angry. I had to take revenge on him. Make him pay. I wanted to punish him for digging up things that didn't belong to him, and for doing it with the help of a Zionist thief. It's possible that her entire goal may just have been to steal Palestinian artifacts to display in her other house in Europe. She could always take refuge there if the security situation deteriorated or even if she was just bored. Any pity I may have felt for him for being stuck with the likes of me soon turned to rage. He and that girl had plundered things that belonged to me. A sly smile crept across my face as I adjusted my scarf around my head and walked up to the first floor of the university building with my friend.

She always used to tease me about my dream of escaping the giant hell of the open-air prison we lived in. And her giggles transformed into all-out laughter as I shared the outline of my escape plan with her. And she kept laughing even when I confessed the details to her. I explained that José was looking to marry a Muslim girl who would help him learn about his new religion, and he was interested in me. To her, this just sounded like a pipe dream, something I'd invented to escape my grim reality ... and my fear of my father. I knew enough to be terrified if I didn't get home by the time he expected. He was constantly threatening to kill me after I'd gotten a reputation around the neighborhood. He even took time off work and used those hours to discipline me instead. I was shamed for daring to dream.

Standing there with my friend, I wished the earth would just open up and swallow me whole. I begged her not to tell the other girls. I wanted to avoid a scandal and didn't want their ridicule. Or José's if it somehow got back to him. She called me crazy. She accused me of being stupid and naïve, of waiting for a knight in shining armor to ride in and save me from my father. But how could I not when he regularly beat me into submission, turning me black and blue as he tried to quell my constant rebellion against him and our whole community?

She made her excuses and went to her French literature class, which was taught by a Belgian professor. I stayed on the balcony alone, looking down over the students crossing through the gate. Watching them, I felt the truth of everything she'd just said: I live in a prison and the only ones with the keys are the soldiers of the occupying army. They alone decide when it opens and closes, who is authorized to enter and exit. Their soldiers and their police dogs closely guard my only ways to escape.

I remember it all. My father kicking my stomach and back. Pulling me out of bed by my hair to make a spectacle of me in front of everyone, as if to reassure them that he had things under control. It was a promise to any girl who chose to follow her gut and rebel that she would be punished publicly, right where she lived. He hit me and spat in my face. Umm Riyala, al-Bilbeisi, and Akram Abu Ras fixed their eyes on my limp body. All this rage because of several phone calls reporting on my bad behavior—refusing to put on the hijab, wearing tight jeans, blatantly disrespecting the neighbors' feelings, or so they said.

I patted at the puffy bruises of my black eyes and inched closer to the classroom door to listen to the French teacher's Belgian accent. I don't understand a word of French. I listened though. The language she was speaking transported me to another, distant world—better than mine—where everyone talks to each other with kindness and compassion. It's a world whose protagonist is a poor man, an orphan with a hunchback living among the giant bells, talking to gargoyles to amuse himself.

I imagined the look on my father's face when he'd receive a photo of me standing there smiling out at him after succeeding in breaking free. As I was busy daydreaming about the bells of Notre Dame and my father's angry face, the security guard closed the main university gate. The professor tapped my shoulder, bringing me back to reality with a start. She smiled. She apologized in English for startling me and suggested that it might be better for me to come indoors where it was warm, rather than stand outside trying to listen in. I was flustered by her sudden offer. I walked into the classroom, eyes lowered to avoid meeting anyone's gaze.

This class was the last spark I needed to fully light the fire inside me to flee the open-air prison I lived in and save myself from inevitable death, before my father discarded me like a rat.

I confided in José how urgently I needed to get out. I felt reassured by him, by the fact that he was a Westerner, a non-Arab Muslim. And he was looking for a Muslim girl. I figured he wouldn't be as closed-minded as most people around us in Gaza were. He helped me get the visa that would completely alter the course of my life. I followed everything up carefully. And my father left. But only after he felt reassured enough that I'd come to my senses and wouldn't stray from the path he'd beat into me with his cane. In the summer of 2001, José and I fled to Madrid.

The apartment we lived in was right in the middle of a block of tall, ugly buildings, on a street whose name I cannot remember. That's because I was born in a neighborhood where refugee homes were built randomly, with no numbers. Our dirt roads and alleys were filled with garbage, stank of urine, and rainy days made the sewage overflow. So I had no idea that streets were supposed to have numbers or that buildings had names and addresses. The first time I'd ever seen an envelope was after I'd moved to Madrid. Where I'm from, messages were passed on by word of mouth, through the children, or communicated directly face-to-face. I was amazed by the order of everything. There were sidewalks for people to walk on. And pedestrians respected signs, obeyed the colors of the traffic lights.

José lived with his parents because life in Madrid was so expensive. This made the small apartment feel even smaller. There were books all over, in every corner, in all the rooms. They were stacked on top of each other, like a climbing plant, branches reaching all the way to the balcony, roots spreading throughout the entire flat. José's father was a historian, which explained his voracious hunger to buy and read so many books. He worked as a professor at the local university after returning from doing research in Morocco.

José went out with his father early every morning, each off to start his own day. I stayed back with his mother María. She did the shopping at the supermarket downstairs, and I stayed upstairs, alone and lonely, with only three meowing cats to keep me company. When they sensed María's footsteps approaching the apartment, their meowing got louder and more annoying. They scampered toward her as soon as she opened the door, and one of them wound its tail around her sheer brown stockings. María spoke to them in a Spanish I didn't understand. She emptied some tin cans into plastic bowls. I noticed the cat's face on the discarded tin and understood that it was cat food. This made me think about the stray cats in the African Quarter back home in Gaza. Boys were always chasing them, pelting them with stones. Umm Riyala poisoned them after they'd run off with the sardines she'd left out and was just about to fry up. And then there was that one cat that al-Bilbeisi sent flying off his roof because she'd peed on his bedsheets. That cat broke a rib and hid in a dark corner, mewling in pain, until she finally died alone.

I sat at the little red kitchen table, where María had put a white bowl filled with colorful plastic fruits. I watched her prepare a breakfast tortilla of egg and potatoes. She thinly sliced Manchego cheese on the side and toasted some bread which she then rubbed with olive oil, garlic, and fresh crushed tomatoes. The warmth of her character shone through in the skill with which she prepared the food. She was in her late fifties, her short hair peppered with gray. Even though we couldn't speak to each other because of the language barrier, I delighted in watching her deftly tie an apron around her waist. I couldn't help but smile at the way she sang as she busily prepared our breakfast. From time to time she tried to pronounce my name, and I corrected her.

"Az ... ma."

"No, no. Asmaa. -ss, not -zz."

"Ah ... Asssmaa."

Beating on her chest and wheezing to act out the meaning of the word, she demonstrated that "asma" in Spanish—as far as I could understand—meant asthma, shortness of breath.

One evening, when José got back, he took me with him to see some of his friends. They were gathered around a table filled with many small plates of food. They called this tapas. Just like what we call mezze. They talked loudly and all at once, creating a pleasantly rowdy atmosphere, and as I couldn't understand a word of what they were saying, I turned my attention to the wide variety of food. I felt how close their food and culture were to ours. There were many different types of olives, as well as grilled peppers and tomatoes. My favorite were the anchovies: small, salty fish smothered in olive oil. I left them to their raucous conversation and turned to tickle a baby strapped into her stroller. Every now and then, her mother rocked her back and forth to stop her crying, picking up the toy that she kept throwing on the floor. I was just like this baby. Neither of us could understand what was going on around us. But she cried and I simply distracted myself with the food.

Later, we made our way back to the apartment, and José told me he was thinking of becoming an imam. He'd decided this after joining a Sufi order in Morocco that had a good number of new Muslims. I was less surprised by José's interest in Islam at this stage of his life than I was at how he and that Jewish Zionist girl had gone ransacking my homeland. But I did feel very disappointed when he shared this new plan with me. I was trying to escape what he wanted to become. So I told him that I couldn't encourage him. I'd experienced my fair share of what hypocritical bearded men could do. Like our Hadith professor at the university who used to terrorize us girls if someone's hijab slid back and revealed so much as a strand of hair. I wondered if the Islam that foreigners practiced could be kinder than ours. Because of their more liberated mentality—or so I thought. I didn't discuss this with him any further. I left him to decide for himself what to do. At the end of the day, I couldn't be the typical Muslim woman with the answer he was looking for. I had come all this way to Spain to be rid of these burdens that had weighed on me since childhood, that I hadn't chosen for myself.

I decided that I had to learn Spanish, to better adapt to his world and communicate with others. When I received my admission letter to the Institute, I jumped for joy, excited to start the following Monday. I started talking to the cats—in Arabic—while I waited for José to come back so I could share the news with him too.

On the first day of class, I met students who'd come to Madrid from all over the world to learn Spanish during their summer holiday. I was happy to connect with other foreigners like me. As evening fell and I waited for José, I walked the city streets, exploring. The next day, I noticed there was a museum behind the Institute. I was so excited; I'd never been inside a museum before. I waited for classes to end and rushed over, but the painting that greeted me was so shocking it stopped me in my tracks. A slaughtered bird. Blood. Head dangling off the edge of a wooden table. It reminded me of the chickens my grandma used to slaughter and pluck herself. I kept walking, quickly. I wanted to see other paintings. The serious people captured inside the frames, looking out at the painter whose brushstrokes had given them stern, strict, unsmiling faces. They were frightening. I was uncomfortable. The somber palette only added to my unease.

I walked up to the next floor. A massive painting commanded my attention. With its many tiny, detailed images inside larger, equally detailed images, it was totally different from those I'd seen downstairs. There were no faces, no bodies, if memory serves me right, but melted clocks of different sizes all across the canvas. I remember an infestation of black ants in one corner. Time stopped. I was no longer aware of where I was or how dark it was getting outside. The black ants drew me into the painting. I started counting them, one by one. Then fingers brushed against my shoulder. Spooked, I jumped back and turned around to see who it was.

"Excuse me, your pencil," a voice said in English.

I clumsily tried to pick my pencil up off the floor, surprised and jolted out of my daze by the man standing there. He was tall and thin with a long black beard and a black hat. I couldn't process what was going on: the last time I'd seen someone who looked like this was at a checkpoint long ago. Had the Mossad sent him here to drag me back to the African Quarter in Gaza? I rubbed my eyes to try and wake myself up—I was sure I had to be seeing things. My intense focus had transformed the ants into this young man. Gesturing toward the painting, he smiled.

"Dalí."

"Huh?"

In English, he repeated, "Dalí. This is a Dalí painting. He's crazy!"

My face turned bright red. I made no effort to hide the fact that I didn't want to be standing there with him. I wished time would stop and save me. I really did have bad luck. My mother always said it had followed me from the moment I was born. Here it was again in this creature clothed in black. Was the neighborhood I left behind not enough for him? I managed to slip away from him and that strange smile that remained plastered on his face even after he saw the fear ripple through my body. I was tongue-tied; I couldn't say a word. I rushed downstairs to save myself. From him. From the head of the slaughtered bird. From the plucked feathers. The swarm of ants that I hadn't even been able to finish counting. I headed back to the café in the Institute, constantly looking over my shoulder to make sure he wasn't following me. I breathed a sigh of relief as I tried to finish studying what we'd covered in class. I waited for José to pick me up. We went back to the apartment. I was safe.

The next evening, I waited for José in the café across from the supermarket near our building. When he arrived, the place was packed. We moved to a table in a quiet corner and ordered two cold bottles of Coke.

I started telling him about my class and what had happened at the museum, but he interrupted me. He took my hand in his and kissed it. He was in good spirits as he blurted out what he had to tell me, his face brimming with boyish enthusiasm. I was excited to hear what he was about to say, but my heart sank when it turned out he wanted to marry me before the end of the month, before my short-stay Schengen visa expired. This brought me right back to the ugliness of my reality. But I pulled myself back together. I knew that I hadn't escaped the chokehold of my neighborhood and my father's authority only to willingly throw myself into another prison. I wasn't going to let someone else suffocate me. Especially not now that I'd seen up close how far he was taking his devotion to religion. His offer of marriage horrified me. And I felt cornered by the need to begin the legal procedures to get Spanish residency. I knew I could only get out of this by running away—from him, from this apartment. Even if it cost me my life.

That night was long and sleepless. I kept tossing and turning, staring at the crucifix hanging over my bed. A picture of José as a child hung next to it. I buried my head in the pillow to quiet my racing thoughts. I'd decided to leave. That was that.

Morning came. I heard the lock turn in the front door—I knew he was gone. I took a shower. Then I picked up my backpack and filled it with my books and papers. I said goodbye to María when she left for the supermarket. Then I headed to the nearby metro station and got off at the stop for the Institute. I waited there, outside the station on the subway steps, anxiously checking my watch.

I spotted him. He was walking toward me, a large bouquet of white roses in hand. I smiled and exhaled in relief. I got into his silver Citroën. I didn't say a word. I focused all my attention on the yellow lines painted on the asphalt and tried to count how many kilometers we'd traveled. Eventually I fell asleep. Nine hours later, we reached the French border. He looked at me and smiled. In English, he said, "We made it to the border! Welcome to France!"

III

Two weeks passed. Jean-Jacques had taken me to Muret in the South of France. He lived in a studio apartment on the top floor of a small four-story building. It was just one room—the kitchen area was inside the main living space. Right in the middle stood a large wooden bookcase. Jean-Jacques had stacked white boxes atop it to separate where he slept from the rest of the apartment. I slept on the sofa bed in the living room.

I met Jean-Jacques when I was working as a war correspondent for the Spanish news agency in Gaza. He was a photojournalist covering the Strip. I helped him out a lot back then. I took him along with me to cover demonstrations and bombings. We'd later stayed in touch by email.

Fairly quickly, though, he told me he was stressed about having me stay in his apartment. He was in the middle of a divorce and his wife would lose it if she found out I was there. He said that she could accuse him of cheating and cause him legal problems.

So I wasn't allowed to make even the faintest noise. He didn't want the neighbors to get suspicious. I was trapped inside, in this new place, in a village I hadn't even been able to see. I spent my days flipping through the huge photo albums he kept stored in those white boxes—anything to kill the time. Sometimes I plugged in my earphones and whispered words in Spanish to echo the recording. I stared out through the skylight at the expanse above. I didn't dare go out alone. I feared that the door would lock behind me and I'd find myself trapped outside. On top of that, I was terrified I might bump into one of the neighbors.

Jean-Jacques promised to take me to the Sunday market. I was so excited when the day finally came. I put on my black floral print cotton dress, laced up my sandals, and tried to tame my unruly hair. He walked out first. He'd told me to wait and go down after him in case any neighbors were around. I closed the door gently then bounced down the stairs. He grabbed my arm to stop me from being so noisy. He was really starting to annoy me, and for a moment I even felt afraid. I knew I had to be more placid. I didn't want him to kick me out. Not in this strange, new part of the world, not when I didn't have a penny to my name.

We walked into the village church together but sat far apart. The priest began reciting hymns that I couldn't understand, despite my attempt to follow along in the little book that was resting right there in front of me on the wooden pew. I saw reverence on the faces of the elderly people surrounding me. I tried to imitate what everyone else was doing—if they sat, I sat, if they stood, I stood. A young woman sat down beside me. She knelt and joined in the prayer. I waited for Jean-Jacques to finish. When he did, he took me by the arm and introduced me to the village priest.

The two of them spoke to each other in French—the only word I could make out was *Palestine*. The priest beamed at me and shook my hand. For a moment, I felt like the Virgin Mary, straight from Palestine, just arrived at this little church to sit among the colorful statues of Christ and Mary that were placed in every corner. The two of them were deep in conversation for some time, so I knelt down on the pew and gazed up at the Virgin. I begged her to send me a sign, anything to save me from the series of misfortunes that was my life.

But nothing came.

Jean-Jacques left the next morning as usual and I stayed in bed, staring up at the sky. I felt anxious and tried to think of a way out of my predicament. I went into the bathroom and emptied the white medicine cabinet of all the pills I could find. I mixed them up and called the emergency number in the kitchen. Then I swallowed them all.

I could hear the ambulance siren. I tried to open my eyes, to be sure of where I was—away from the apartment, away from Jean-Jacques. I needed to know I was somewhere safe. Through a haze, I could make out the features of a young nurse. Looking up at him, I placed my hand on my chest, felt my beating heart, and mumbled, "They killed him ... they killed Abdullah."

IV

Judith woke me up for breakfast. Later, she helped me out of my clothes so I could shower. I shuddered when she ran the cold water over my back and shoulders and I signaled to her to make the water warmer. The bar of soap slipped from my hand and she helped me pick it up. I finished my shower and put on my green hospital gown, open in the back. I returned to the room I shared with Chantal. She was lying on her right side, as usual, smiling in my direction. It was time for Judith to disinfect my wrist, so she cut a piece of gauze to wrap around the wound. I took my pill and tried to relax on the bed.

I felt comfortable, safe, at the Saint-Simon residence, a *maison de repos*, they called it. I hadn't felt that way since I'd fled Gaza for Madrid—then Madrid for France, and now Jean-Jacques for here. I couldn't communicate with any of the nurses because of the language barrier. Or maybe it was the severe psychological trauma that had left me unable to speak.

Talking to me in broken English, the young doctor tried to help me dig through my memories to locate the source of my sudden inability to speak, to understand why I broke down in uncontrollable sobs every time I saw him. I tried to revisit the past but was overwhelmed by the painful memories that flooded my consciousness. Like the shock of the moment I saw the dead body of the boy I was in love with as a girl printed on his death notice. Abdullah ... Or the time my dad tried to kill me by throwing a huge gas canister at me and then beat me up in front of the whole neighborhood. The doctor encouraged me to make art to alleviate my depression. So I took on drawing and sculpting. Other times, I sat on a green wooden bench in the garden and watched the nurses stroll around with other patients. I always turned my face to the sun, trying to soak up as much warmth as I could.

I even indulged in a little love affair with another patient. It relieved the side effects of my medication but also the weight of my memories. We crept off together to the creek that ran through the grounds at the edge of the residence. He talked to me about his daughter. He wasn't allowed to see her because he was an alcoholic. Frederic gifted me a picture of a brown horse galloping through tall green grass. On the back, he'd written in English, *For your free soul, wherever you go, stay free as you are*. I still carry it with me today.

V

Three weeks into my stay at Saint-Simon, a social worker helped me find a free shelter to move into. Claire Maison, a publicly funded women's shelter in the Saint-Cyprien neighborhood of Toulouse, had single and shared rooms available for battered women and those suffering from psychological trauma due to violence, poverty, and war.

I ticked all those boxes, so I was accepted into the shelter. It felt so good to finally be able to live in a room that was my own. I wouldn't have to share it with anyone. I would get my own key. It would give me privacy, and no one would be able to intrude on my space. It would be somewhere new—quiet and safe—where I could just live. Without war, without any of the nosy neighbors and their prying eyes. I'd go to sleep in my own little space where my noisy sisters, my father's TV, and my mother's shouting couldn't reach me. I would protect myself with this space that was mine. I wouldn't have to put up with the whims of any man.

With the help of Mademoiselle Sylvia, a social worker at the shelter, I started learning French. She'd been helping me manage my personal affairs and paperwork. She was the one who'd introduced me to Nathalie, my lawyer. The French classes bored me. They were meant for people who couldn't read or write. But they were free. I spent my class time scribbling down new words in my notebook.

Slowly, my relationships with the women around me began to deepen. But I still couldn't speak. If I needed to communicate, I used my hands. I still remember two of the women well. My next-door neighbor, who was born with a limp in her left leg. And Magdalena, from Tanzania, who spoke such rapid-fire English that I could barely understand a thing she said.

Later, I got to know Nakhla, an Algerian woman whose room was on the upper floor. She worked as a house cleaner and came back late every day. She was plump, with a round face and charcoal-colored hair. During Ramadan, she'd take me to the Arnaud Bernard market to buy vegetables, and also to the Arab neighborhood. That's where she bought halal meat. Nakhla was like a big sister to me. She was always cheerful and spoke to me in Egyptian Arabic so I could understand her better. She even helped me find some work under the table as a server in a Moroccan restaurant. I needed some freedom from the shelter's strict rules. And before winter came, she took me to the Emmaüs charity shop so I could get some winter clothes for cheap.

VI

Every Monday morning, after I made breakfast, I went to the MJC Roguet Saint-Cyprien youth center. It wasn't far from the shelter. That's where I met Rosario, the center's public relations coordinator. She was Spanish and I stammered my way through conversations in Spanish and English with her; I'd started taking intensive sessions with the shelter's speech therapist, who was helping me regain my ability to speak. With Rosario, I felt for the first time that someone could understand the difficulty I was going through as a recent immigrant. Maybe because she was the eldest daughter of a Spanish immigrant who'd come to Toulouse fleeing Franco's rule. I met her father, Javier, the first time she invited me over to her place. She lived in Saint-Cyprien, near where she worked.

Looking at him, I don't know why I saw my grandfather in his features. He told me the story of how he had sought refuge here in Toulouse. He'd fled Spain for this border town on foot, crossing the Pyrenees with his wife and children. He talked about the French racism that he and his comrades had endured after escaping Franco to save their lives. They were just like the stories of suffering that I'd heard from both my grandfathers— my dad's dad, the Bedouin, and my mom's dad, the farmer.

In 1948, they also had to flee their villages. They walked all the way to Gaza. They'd also faced discrimination—from the original citizens of Gaza, and from other refugees coming from Palestinian cities like Haifa and Jaffa. Perhaps it was fate that willed me to remain haunted by these experiences, no matter how far I traveled. There I was, by chance, talking to a Spanish elder about his suffering under Franco and how he too had to seek asylum far from his own homeland.

VII

I'd been living at Claire Maison for about a year and had begun taking classes where Rosario worked, at the art center affiliated with MJC Roguet, when I met Catherine. She was French, of Portuguese descent, and worked as the center's cultural coordinator. With time, we became good friends, and through her I met French people my own age who were socially mainstream—that is to say, people without major psychological trauma or a difficult past. They were the kind of twenty-somethings who spent their time forming bands and playing music in bars and nightclubs.

Their heavily accented English was mixed with French and I couldn't make out everything they said. They were curious about my story, and their curiosity somehow made me feel like I'd landed there from Mars. They showed a genuine interest in what was happening in Palestine and expressed their political and intellectual concern for the plight of the Palestinian people, but this put me in the awkward position of feeling I couldn't tell them about the cruelty I'd suffered at the hands of Palestinians in the camps where I'd grown up. So I just nodded along as they offered their sympathy. What had happened to me shouldn't affect people's perception of the Palestinian cause or obscure the suffering of the entire Palestinian people.

So I decided to keep my suffering to myself and not say anything. They took me to a big concert that some leftists organized every year to showcase French bands of Arab origin. They were mostly from the Maghreb, and their music spoke about the struggles of immigrants and refugees in France. There I was, trying to escape my own tragedy and live some kind of a normal life. But to the people around me, my life would never be seen through any other lens. I was forced to remain trapped between a miserable past I'd never wanted and a leftist present focused on the suffering of immigrants in France. Basically, my quest to find some inner peace— even if only for a few days—had landed me right in the heart of everything I'd tried to disavow.

The concert began. The first band was called Beur, sounding like the French word for butter. It was verlan slang, reversing the two syllables of the word for Arab. Mixing French and North African Arabic words in their lyrics, they rapped over hip-hop beats about the racism they experienced as Maghrebi youth in France.

Catherine translated the songs and their meanings for me: they were singing about how the government refused to recognize their communities even though they'd fought on the front lines to defend France in World War II. She was so enthusiastic telling me this. I just smiled back at her.

Standing in the crowd, I shouted at a young man who'd dropped his beer on the fur coat I'd bought for three euros at the Emmaüs charity shop. Everyone was packed in tight, trying to keep their drinks from spilling on each other. Suddenly, they all started jumping up and down and chanting along with the band, "Wallah, wallah, wallah." I thought their accents were charming. I moved away from the crowd to avoid getting beer poured on my head. And when I heard the fireworks go off, I instinctively ducked under a big wooden picnic table. It sounded like rockets bombing Gaza.

We all left at around two in the morning and went to Catherine's friend Fabrice's apartment. Everyone snacked on chips and nuts, and we carried on drinking wine and Heinekens. I sank into the sofa and drifted off—I was exhausted. When I woke up the next morning, I walked back to my quiet room at the shelter.

VIII

I met Bernard through Catherine. He was six years older than me, tall, with an athletic build and sandy brown hair. He was always talking to me about the political issues he was reading about in the left-wing French magazine *Marianne* and how important he thought it was that the Palestinians should come to an agreement with the Israelis. He insisted that peace was the only solution. This made it clear to me that I would never be able to escape what I represented to these people. The way they profiled me—Palestinian, immigrant, woman, fleeing war. Everyone ignored that I was a human first, above all else, and that, as a human, I too have the right to escape my past for very personal reasons. Even if they seem trivial, they are important to me.

I tried repeatedly to explain my thought process to Bernard. To no avail. Over and over, I said that I had come here for one simple reason—to find a few inches of calm, a safe space—to live like an ordinary person with no extraordinary abilities. I wanted him to understand that I hadn't left the Gaza neighborhood I grew up in to carry my national cause in my back pocket. Nor to shape myself into the image of a militant woman of the Palestinian resistance. I left to find some personal space, a few square meters of my own where I could put a bed and a table. When I stretched out in the little bed in my room at the shelter, I thought about writing a children's book. It would be about a girl who trapped a caterpillar in a glass jar. She put leaves inside for it to eat and poked holes in the cover to let in some air. She watched it closely every day, waiting for it to spin its cocoon and then turn into a butterfly. She waited for it to spread its wings and fly away.

IX

I married Bernard in June 2003. It was unusually hot for France, one of the hottest days of the year. Nearly three thousand elderly people died alone in their apartments. True to form, my bad luck continued to follow me every time I tried to start a new chapter in my life.

I chose a dress in ruby red because I didn't want to be a traditional bride all dressed in white. I donned elbow-length beige gloves and a matching hat. Synthetic roses held a delicate veil that fell over my face. The heat and humidity were suffocating, and my dress and its long train clung uncomfortably to my body. The second we were done with the wedding photos, I ripped off my hat and satin gloves and changed into a cotton dress I could dance in. I didn't once think about my family. I felt proud for having decided to marry a man I'd chosen for myself and not waiting for my father's approval. Everyone danced and was merry, drinking wine into the early hours of dawn. I drank and danced with them all night, though I couldn't understand what they were saying in French. And because I wasn't used to drinking, I got drunk really quickly. I jumped into the pool in my dress for some relief from the suffocating heat. I wrapped myself in a silk shawl that was lying under a table and fell asleep on the grass next to the pool while Bernard sang and danced with his friends.

I'd gotten married because I'd decided I needed a rest. A little break from running away, from moving from one country, one emotional state to another. I must have broken some family record for trauma and displacement. I was sick of always feeling like I had to prove my identity to others. And tired of conversations that more often than not ended with people saying that I had to understand the struggles of Israelis, who suffered from the situation just like I did. I didn't want to hear about how I had to be more like Gandhi, how I, and other Palestinians, should stop the attacks, the armed resistance. How I had to do my best to try to achieve peace—like they do. I just repeated, over and over again, that my fleeing had nothing to do with my grandparents' right of return or reclaiming the homeland they'd been expelled from. I hadn't fled to make a peace deal or make anyone feel sorry for me. All I wanted was a space of my own, a few square meters where I could put a bed and a table.

X

We traveled, Bernard and I, after our June wedding. We fled July's sweltering heat for a series of little French villages called Gorges du Tarn, perched alongside a river in the South of France. I was unbelievably happy as we strolled together through the narrow alleyways. The streets were paved with even rows of cobblestones, balconies were filled with roses, doors were painted blue, pink, and burgundy red. Sunday mornings we shopped at the farmers market for vegetables and meat, tasting olives as we browsed through the stands.

I felt more comfortable in these villages than I had in Toulouse, where I lived with Bernard. I liked the hardwood floors in the houses. It was quiet, a place where I finally felt safe, happy. For our holiday, we had rented a white limestone house with gray shale inner walls. Time stopped there. I still remember the thick white cotton bedsheets and the bouquets of dried lavender hanging in the closets. I'll never forget that fragrance. Nor the taste of jam spread on a toasted baguette. Even the coffee was more delicious there, nothing like the plain coffee that my mother used to prepare in a tin pot, constantly taking it off the fire so it wouldn't boil over onto the gas burner that was covered with aluminum foil to keep it clean. After our breakfasts at the wooden table for two, we spent our days visiting the village. I felt good inside myself. I felt proud of my decision to run away that night. I'd gotten myself here.

Happiness coursed through my veins deep into my soul. I breathed fresh, clean air. I loved looking at the many different kinds and colors of vegetables. It was the first time that I'd ever seen fields so green. It was the first time that I'd felt such an affinity to a calm, simple place, a place where I could belong.

XI

It was the last day of June 2001, an unusually quiet Saturday. I'd decided to run away with José. At four in the morning, we set out to take a yellow taxi to the Egyptian border. I took one last look back at my sister Amal through the rear window.

My mind was a muddle of joy and despair. I laughed and cried. I wanted to hold José close, but the driver's nosiness stopped me. And I was sure that Umm Riyala was sneaking looks at me from behind her curtains.

We finally arrived at the Rafah border crossing. Other travelers were sitting on the ground, spread out all around. Like us, they were waiting for their fate to be decided. They were going to Egypt for work, or medical treatment, or to visit their families. I felt my anxiety levels rise when a woman told me she'd been waiting for the permit to cross the border for fifteen days already. She'd decided to come back to the exact same spot every morning with food and drink to last the day. I glanced over at José, who hadn't left my side. He didn't go over to the foreigners' transit area. He stayed with me and all the other travelers holding Egyptian-issued refugee documents. I sat next to the woman I'd met, waiting for our turn to cross.

I was stuck there, swatting away the flies landing on my face, until a border guard wearing a Palestinian Authority uniform approached us. I bolted upright, José too. The officer started talking to him like I didn't even exist. He told José to go into his office, behind the fence. But José refused to go without me. The officer agreed to let me go with him. We walked into the large office together. There were other Palestinian officers there. On the wall hung photos of Yasser Arafat—one with Abu Jihad, another shaking hands with that same officer. He asked me disdainfully, "What are you doing with him?"

"He's my fiancé. We're going to get married in Spain."

"Fiancé, is he?" His sarcasm was evident.

"Yeah. His name is José Abdel Noor. He's Muslim."

"Live and learn …"

A malicious smile crept across his lips as he said this. This worried José. He immediately intervened and asked what was going on. Right away, the nosy officer stopped interrogating me and handed José his passport along with my travel document and Schengen visa.

We made our way to another border taxi and crossed through the Palestinian checkpoint into the occupation one. We stood in an endless line as we waited for the soldier to call out our names and return our documents. Tension was thick in the air, people's fear palpable. Hints of both were visible on everyone's faces, mine included. Stoic, we all tried to appear as neutral as possible, showing no distress that could possibly aggravate the occupation soldiers. We knew this could complicate our travel and ruin our hopes of leaving. But we'd been waiting for hours and I really needed to pee. Finally the soldier released me; he called my name to come and collect my travel document. I rushed up to him and he shot at the ground right by my foot. I froze, terrified, my heart racing. Another soldier came forward, his rifle pointed straight at me, barking in broken Arabic, "Go back, go back."

I went limp and struggled to drag my body back to my place in the line. Swallowing with difficulty, I wiped the sweat pooling on my forehead. The soldier threw my papers on the ground. I waited until he'd backed away before picking them up.

I entered the inspection room alone, without José. I was terrified at the idea that we would be kept apart, that he might be forced to travel on without me. But my fears were assuaged when I saw him waiting for me by the side of the bus that would take us across into Egypt. The occupation soldier boarded the bus. I looked at José and smiled. We were finally getting out of this place. After all the physical and psychological torture I'd experienced in the neighborhood, we would finally be able to relax.

But then everything came shattering down. Time started moving in the wrong direction. The soldier was ordering us all off the bus because the Egyptian checkpoint had closed for the day. Anger twisted itself up inside me, rising through my throat up into my nose, choking me. I exploded when the soldier walking through the bus got to my seat.

"I'm not moving. I'm not getting off this bus. You'll have to shoot me first!"

José tried to calm me down and convince me that my anger wouldn't change anything—it might actually make it more difficult for us to cross. He picked me up and lifted me over his shoulder. I kicked at his stomach to try to break free, which only made him tighten his grip around my legs to stop me wiggling. As he carried me away from the border control area, I glared back at the soldier, who was lifting the visor of his helmet.

Back on the Palestinian side, I turned away from José. I refused to speak to him or even look at him. He promised that we could sleep right there on the ground, so we could be the first to get a morning border taxi. And as he promised, we managed to cross the border that morning. We immediately took another taxi directly to the airport in Cairo. I couldn't contain my delight when I heard the driver's Egyptian accent. I hugged José close. He smiled and hugged me back. I dozed off on his shoulder to Abdel Halim Hafez singing about the fortune teller, *Your skies are full of rain, and your way forward is blocked ... it's blocked.*

PART TWO
RETURN

I

Whenever I asked her about the night I was born, my mother always said, "Akh. What can I tell you? When you were born, the rain nearly drowned us and all the sewers in the neighborhood overflowed."

She would pause, recalling the terror of those moments. I could never get her to talk, to tell me more about that night. Had it not been for the noisy chatter of the neighborhood women, I would never have heard the story of my birth, with all its different—and sometimes even conflicting—details.

Despite the varied accounts, all agreed that that night in the Gaza Strip had been bad luck—I was a survivor of the flooding of Shuja'iya.

After all of al-Sakakini's children emigrated to America, my father rented a room from him.

Back then, everybody in our neighborhood burrowed inside late at night. Only Abu Ibrahim's donkey remained outside on the muddy street, tethered to the doorstep right next to the window of our little room.

Umm Rashid the midwife arrived, out of breath from having run over with my father, who'd gone to fetch her. As she worked hard to relieve my mother's labor pains and deliver me safely, the neighbors' complaints about the sewage overflowing into their bathrooms began to reach a fever pitch. Holding lanterns to light their path, everyone gathered at Abu Ibrahim's house for his help cleaning and sanitizing their houses.

Abu Ibrahim sold Clorox and nitric acid, which people called fire water. In the neighborhood, people used it to disinfect their toilets after every use. He hitched his wooden cart to his donkey's back and walked through the whole area, house by house, to clear away the sewage and disinfect them.

Meanwhile, Umm Rashid was scrambling to save me. My face was blue from lack of oxygen, the umbilical cord wrapped around my neck. She smacked my tender flesh with the palm of her hand, turning the blue a healthy pink. I wailed to silence the donkey that hadn't stopped braying throughout my entire delivery.

When he heard me cry, my father burst through the door, "My child is here!"

"Congratulations, God has blessed you with a fourth beautiful little girl. May your family live a long, prosperous life."

My father frowned. A dark shadow cast over his face. He retreated from the room, clapping his hands together in disbelief at his bad luck of having found a wife who could only give him daughters.

One time, my mother was more willing to talk about the night of my birth. But my father's father, Harb Abu Diab, cut her off:

"Our family's had nothing but bad luck since you came around."

And then he started recounting the details of that fateful day when he'd gone to ask my other grandfather for my mother's hand. He and his family originally hailed from Al Naqb Desert, but my mom, Hind, was the daughter of a village farmer. He would tell us that story all the time. Even more often than the story of how he'd been expelled from his land, and how my Qatatwi grandma, Hadbaa, had lost her mind when she walked all the way from Al Naqb to Gaza on foot, ending up a refugee.

He rested the copper teakettle on the lit brazier in the room where he and my grandmother slept. He left it to boil until it became dark and bitter. We listened to the crackling of the wood and the sound the teapot lid made as he slid it off to pour tea into a little glass cup. Then he poured it back into the kettle, repeating this process a number of times until the leaves settled at the bottom. And then he drank it, still telling the tale of how he decided to visit Grandpa Abu Shanab's house to ask for one of his daughters' hand in marriage.

My Grandpa Salah Abu Shanab found marrying off my mother to be the perfect solution. Even if it was to a Sabawi Bedouin from Beersheba. He would have one less mouth to feed, one less reminder of his poverty and misfortune. And my Grandpa Abu Diab insisted on my father being married off as soon as humanly possible. Even if it was to the daughter of a peasant, a rural farmer. There'd been rumors that his son had been caught peeping at the neighborhood women as they bathed.

Grandpa Abu Diab said he cursed the day when al-Bilbeisi, who owned the corner store, showed him where Abu Shanab lived after he'd lost his way:

"Walk out of the shop and take the dirt road on the right. You will see the border buses, they have Abu Elbeh written on the side. Keep walking straight down for 200 more meters. When you smell roses, follow the scent. It will lead you right to his doorstep."

My grandfather paused. He sipped his tea, forefinger slightly raised, eyes fixed on the tin roof. He placed his teacup back on the thin metal tray. The four of us girls sat all around him in silence. We gazed at his slender brown face, round hazel eyes, and an Adam's apple made more prominent by his frailness. We hung on every last detail of his story, chuckling at how he made fun of our mother and her family.

Grandpa Abu Diab continued his story. He knocked on the large iron gate. After ten minutes, no one had come. So he knocked again, more forcefully, so that Abu Shanab would hear him. Soon after, he heard heavy footsteps approaching. Two eyes peered out at him from behind the iron gate. Hands cleared away the leaves that covered the slits in the gate and prevented visitors from seeing inside. Abu Shanab was there, asking:

"Hello? Who's there?"

"Yes, yes, hello. I'm your neighbor Harb Abu Diab. I come with well wishes."

Abu Shanab put the key into the lock and started fiddling with it left and right, pulling the door hard to one side to open it. He appraised the stranger at his doorstep, taking in his thin frame, gray jellabiya, and black agal holding his white hetta in place on his head.

"Welcome, please come in."

"Thank you. The pleasure is mine."

Abu Shanab regularly received guests in the sitting area outside. People came to him looking for help to solve their problems and disputes. The little council area he'd set up looked out over his garden. It was covered with dried palm fronds, Damascene jasmine climbing over a wooden trellis. He gestured to Abu Diab to take a seat beside him on a handmade wicker chair. Then Grandpa Abu Diab presented his request, putting a definitive end to the doubts visible on Abu Shanab's face as to the purpose of his visit.

"Without beating around the bush, mukhtar, I have come to you with a request to bring our lineages closer together."

Sheer joy lit up Grandpa Abu Shanab's face, but only for a moment. He quickly forced his features to settle back into their usual sternness and furrowed his brow, his wrinkles deepening.

"Where are your people from?"

"We are Bani Attiyas from the Tiyaha tribe in Sabaa, Beersheba."

"Welcome. We welcome the goodness and blessings you're bringing with you."

All Abu Shanab could think of was how getting rid of one of his daughters would surely bring the same good luck to her sisters. He would pass on the burden and responsibility of looking out for her to another man.

Abu Diab, on the other hand, was thinking that the village woman's peasant origins wouldn't anger the men of the Tiyaha tribe. He himself had married a Qatatwi woman who traced her own origins to the Bedouin of the Egyptian Sinai. He knew that the man would never be faulted for this by either his family or his tribe. Marriage, even to the daughter of a farmer, was better than continual complaints about his only son's reputation.

That day, Abu Shanab chose my mother, Hind. He picked her because she'd never finished primary school. By the time they met, she'd already started to panic because she was afraid she'd end up like her older sister. Zahana was notoriously a spinster, and my grandfather had been compelled to marry her off to the neighborhood idiot.

My mother feared she too would become a local laughingstock with a husband boys threw rocks at.

She also worried about what she'd heard Grandma Amneh say about Bedouin men—how they were not to be trusted because of their wandering eyes, their love for women, and wanting children with them all. But despite how anxious she was—and how young—her strict father left her no choice but to accept this offer of marriage.

My mother never saw my father's face until the wedding ceremony itself, when she walked into the little room he'd rented in the al-Sakakini's house. The newlyweds would live in that one room for the first years of their marriage. But when my older sisters and I were born, it got too cramped for us all. So my father decided to move in with my Abu Diab grandparents in the African Quarter.

This new house was principally made up of two rooms: one for receiving guests and another they'd further divided in two by hanging a curtain from a clothesline. A narrow hallway extended from the front door to the kitchen at the other end. There were two bathrooms on the right, one with just a toilet and the other to bathe in. The roof was covered with a sheet of tin, which made it hotter in the summer and leaked rain in the winter. When guests came to visit, my mother spread out a straw mat to cover the cement floor. And she hosed down the cement with cold water every day, to cool it off.

My grandfather built this house after he'd moved my Grandma Hadbaa and my father from where he used to live in the Nuseirat refugee camp south of Gaza City to the African Quarter. He'd found work in the city center as a night watchman in a government school.

The houses in the neighborhood were cramped and crowded. Refugees had been crammed into them like sardines packed together into little tins. The residents of the camps, my mother included, believed that the Israelis had a hand in this. The close living quarters, where everyone could hear everything—big or small—made it easier to spy and catch the fedayeen.

Al-Jalaa Street is a main thoroughfare that separates the homes of the citizens of Gaza from the homes of refugees. The neighborhood called the African Quarter is located right at the end of al-Jalaa Street and a dirt road there separates the homes of refugees from Afro-Palestinians, keeping them apart.

I grew up with my sisters, Kifah, Amal, and Sabreen, in our grandfather's house, to the sounds of our neighbors' quarrels. Daughters-in-law arguing with mothers-in-law, husbands with wives. The eyes of the neighborhood ladies, sitting on their doorsteps, tracked everyone. They only ever moved when the green Israeli army patrol jeeps rolled down the street. My grandfather's house was surrounded by the homes of the Abu Riyala, Abu Kirsh, and Abu Ayman families. The Abu Aymans' house had been deserted since they'd left.

My mother covered the big metal door to our house with a blanket, so that we could leave it open without the neighbors being able to snoop on us.

My father soon found a job as an auto mechanic in a Jewish-owned garage. He joined the ranks of the many other neighborhood men who worked inside 48-Palestine all week and only came back on weekends and Jewish holidays.

He got this job after completing a training course at an UNRWA-affiliated institute. So he left my mother alone most of the time to look after the house and all of us. She had us four to take care of as well as Grandma Hadbaa, who was a handful. My grandfather was out a lot too, because of his job as a night watchman at the local school.

In the mornings, our mom left our eldest sister, Kifah, in charge. Carrying a red plastic basket on her head, she would go to buy vegetables from the market stalls in Shuja'iya. I made the most of the time she was out, dodging Kifah to run off and meet my friends—who were all boys. I lied to her and claimed I was going to play out back and pick mallow for our mother to cook. She believed me in good faith. But what I was actually doing was meeting the boys in Abu Ayman's deserted courtyard. I took care to jump over the wall to get there so Umm Riyala couldn't spot me.

We used to meet up on Fridays after prayer time, once the worshippers went home to nap and we'd finished our homework. The boys snuck cigarettes. I'd proved my bravery to them by sneaking out of the house without my mother knowing, earning me the nickname Nus Nseis. He was the hero of our childhood stories. Our mothers told us all about how naughty and clever he was, always managing to escape the ghoul who wanted to eat him. Like Nus Nseis, 1 also found ways to get myself out of trouble if my mom ever did catch me misbehaving.

II

Rami always made fun of how I dressed. He worked at the sewing factory my dad's Christian friend Saad al-Sarif owned. And still my mother refused to let me wear jeans or trousers—they're for boys, she always said. Whenever I got my cotton dresses dirty or ripped my woolen tights, she'd insist on washing them even if that meant I'd have to wear them damp and torn in the bitter cold of winter.

Whenever she made me wear that red-and-blue plaid cotton dress, I felt like I was suffocating. It buttoned all the way up to my neck, and I couldn't take it off without my sisters' help. We were the only kids dressed like that, and our mom bragged about how pretty our dresses were—our dad used to get them from the Souq al-Bala flea market, inside the 1948 areas.

My mom spent her time proving her superiority over the other women in the neighborhood. She was proud of her tidiness and cleanliness, of the scent of Tide washing powder that wafted from the clothes she pinned to the clothesline outside our window. She didn't let me cut my hair short—like a boy—or ride a bicycle like the other children my age on our block. Instead, she pulled it back tightly into a candy-colored hairband decorated with a plastic bauble. She practically tore my head from my shoulders while tying a ponytail so tight that not one hair could escape.

On holidays and special occasions, she'd give us French braids, a hairstyle she'd once seen on an Israeli woman, a soldier who was patrolling the street in front of our house. During the year, when lice spread around our school, the real torture began. That's when she really started pulling and combing. She doused our heads with kerosene, and we had to endure it for two long days and nights of house arrest. She then passed a sharp, fine-toothed bone comb from our scalp to the end of our hair. She repeated the process several times until she was sure they were completely gone.

My relationship with Rami was getting weird and fluctuated according to his moods. Sometimes he'd sneak me his bike, though it was too big for me, so I could surreptitiously practice riding it. Other times, he looked right past me and talked only to the other boys, ignoring me completely. He even asked them to exclude me from the group. No girls allowed, he said.

He was a teenager already, five years older than me—tall and handsome. He had a mole on his right cheek and dimples when he smiled. His eyes were a dreamy shade of hazel that suited his dark brown skin, and he'd style his jet-black hair with gel when he came to meet us in the subbar cactus grove. Rami liked to show off his blue cotton shirt. He left the top buttons undone, letting us see a bit of his chest. He never missed a chance to remind us that because he worked in Saad al-Sarif's sewing factory, he sewed his own pair of jeans, the kind none of us could afford. Only Israelis could, and they were only sold in their shops. Rami was stubborn. He never could do things in half-measures. He didn't mind being beaten by soldiers every time he threw stones at them. During confrontations with the occupation army, he masked up and set up roadblocks of burning tires with other boys his age. We could see how he relished the retelling of how he'd managed to land a Molotov cocktail he'd thrown right on an Israeli army jeep. Yet despite how bravely he faced the occupation soldiers, he was truly afraid of our neighbor, Nidal Abu Riyala. His eyes burned if you mentioned Nidal in front of him.

Nidal Abu Riyala lived in the African Quarter, right across from us. He and his father worked as neighborhood garbage collectors. I was terrified at the mere sight of him and immediately averted my gaze to avoid his. Nidal had a burn scar on the right side of his neck, just below his chin. The whites of his eyes shone brightly in the dark, like when the Israelis cut off our electricity supply. We all suspected that he'd been the one who started the sewing factory fire at the al-Shati refugee camp, to get back at Rami. I used to see him lounging around on a bamboo chair, drinking tea, showing off a razor blade between his teeth and threatening the local boys that he'd cut them if they so much as came near him. He tracked me every time I snuck out to meet Rami, Abdullah, and the rest of our crew in the grove.

One Friday morning when I was about to go meet up with everyone, Nidal appeared right next to me. I was so startled I couldn't budge. I wished the earth would open up and swallow me whole. Or that someone would come out of the mosque and see me. I looked down at the ground, breathing hard, my chest rising and falling anxiously. Nidal flung mud at my dress. "Look at me—what are you afraid of?"

Reluctantly, I did as he said. I worried that if I didn't, he would slash my face with his razor blade. He started toward me, holding a dead rat by the tail and dangling it in front of me. I was so terrified I peed my pants. I flew back into the house. He laughed behind me. I never did feel safe around him. And I never liked it when my mother sent me out late to buy her things. I found it reassuring that Abdullah, who was Rami's brother, was always nearby, keeping watch. He whistled from his balcony; I knew that I was safe.

Rami and Abdullah's mom became friends with my mom after her husband left her. He married a woman from Jerusalem, got his Jerusalem ID, and lived out his life on the Green Line. Our moms consoled each other and helped each other out in times of crisis. Silently, my feelings for Abdullah grew. But he was an idiot who couldn't tell that I liked him. I swooned whenever my mom sent me over to borrow some Tide or their wooden broom, because I would get to see him and we could set the date for our next rendezvous in the cactus grove. Later, I also found out that he would be walking me to school. My mother was getting increasingly worried about the occupation soldiers. We were hearing more and more stories about girls being kidnapped, raped, and murdered.

When my father came home from work, I knew my mother would be distracted, so I could run off to catch up with Abdullah. He knew to wait for me at the end of the alley.

One day, I managed to slip away from my mother and also avoided Nidal, but I got stuck talking to al-Bilbeisi who was sitting in his corner shop.

He called out to me from his little chair. A breeze lifted the single strand of hair covering his bald spot, and he tried to smooth it back down. He sat in his makeshift office, behind a plank of wood that he lifted to monitor who was walking in and out, suspicious we'd shoplift.

"Where are you off to, ammo?"

"I'm just here to buy an ice cream."

"Your dad back yet?"

"Yes, a little while ago. He's so tired he went straight to bed."

"How's your mom? She OK?"

"Yes, she's fine, she said to say hi."

He put on his glasses. He then licked his finger and thumbed through the pages of his notebook to the page labeled "Hind's daughters." He recorded my purchase, adding to our tab. I thanked him and left.

"Bye ammo, don't forget to say hi to your dad from me. And don't play with the boys, eh? Rami's been acting out the past couple of days."

I moved out of his line of sight and toward the dusty street at the end of our alley, where Abdullah was already waiting for me. We ran to the grove to join Rami and the rest of the kids. We played until sunset. We went back together, and Abdullah dropped me off where we'd met earlier. My mother greeted me with my grandpa's crutch, which usually hung on the doorframe.

"Where have you been? Do you know what time it is? Just you wait until your father wakes up. Hurry up now, go shower and change out of those clothes, you're filthy!"

The sunset call to prayer was filtering in through the tiny bathroom window as I went in. The brass water heater gurgled along with it. My mother came in to adjust the settings and closed the window. The smell of kerosene was suffocating.

She rubbed my back thoroughly with natural Nabulsi olive oil soap, scrubbing it with a loofa dipped in a bowl in which she'd mixed boiling hot water with cold water from the tap. The little bathroom was warm and cozy. Mom called my sisters in and washed our hair one after the other to save on hot water. After bath time was over, we put on our long cotton nightdresses and rushed to get into our bed. It was on the ground, covering the little holes of the dirt floor caused by rinse water from the bathroom. We rubbed our feet against each other to get warm again.

Our mother pulled a heavy duvet cover, stuffed with our summer clothes, over us. Its weight made it hard to breathe. We slept huddled around her, fighting to be the closest to her. She turned off the light and told us the story of Jbene, the girl whose skin was as white as cheese. The other girls were so jealous of her complexion that they took her to a grove and strung her up off a branch of a sycamore tree, leaving her there for a ghoul to come and eat her. But she managed to get back to her house because a prince on horseback found her and took her home.

My sisters fell fast asleep. But I kept tossing and turning, trying to get comfortable. I couldn't get the ghoul out of my mind. I kept seeing Nidal's face—he morphed into the ghoul; he swallowed me whole. I hid my face under the heavy covers. The soothing whir of my mother's sewing machine eventually lulled me to sleep.

III

Amal shook me awake that morning.

"Get up, quick. Abdullah's here. He's asking for you—I think something's happened."

I rubbed my eyes and stumbled over to the door.

"What are you doing here? What's wrong? What if my dad wakes up and sees you? He'll beat me up! Go away!"

"Hurry up, get dressed. Come to the grove. All hell is breaking loose. Rami and Nidal are about to kill each other!"

I couldn't help but feel scared. I knew how violent Nidal was, that he didn't play fair. I also knew about his thinly concealed hatred for Rami.

"Fine, just give me a minute. I'll come up with something."

I splashed cold water on my face from the yellow plastic bowl that we kept in the sink. I undid the elastic band that my mother had tied around a bunch of mint and pulled my loose hair back in it. Then I barged through the wooden door to the small living room. I found my dad laid out on a mattress on the floor, dead asleep.

Out of nowhere, my mom's sandal flew at me.

"You little monster, what are you doing here? Your father needs his rest. Go outside and play."

I didn't hesitate. Abdullah was still waiting for me, and we ran off to the grove. We got there and saw Nidal lying face down on the ground. Evil fury drained from Rami's face as he kicked and stomped on Nidal with all his might. He spat on him.

"I'll cut out your tongue, you bastard. Your sister's a whore and you're trash, you and your whole family!"

Abdullah and I tried to intervene and get Rami to calm down. He looked at me with eyes so red they were about to explode with rage.

"Get out of here. Who said you could come?"

I held my ground. But, afraid of him, I didn't dare move. Nidal seized his chance to wriggle free of Rami's grip.

He limped away and hid among the cacti. The blood dripping from his head stained the thorny green plants red. Rami yanked the subbar fruits off, indifferent to their constant little prickles, and flung them at Nidal. Then he turned back toward Abdullah and shouted, "Take her back to her house—now! I can't stand the sight of her!" He stormed off, got on his bicycle, and disappeared.

Abdullah took my hand and brushed the tears from my cheek, "Don't take it personally. Something's been up with him the past two days. Angry at everyone and everything!"

He walked me all the way back to my house and said goodbye. I couldn't shake off how scared I was by what I'd seen—the fury that had taken hold of Rami's face.

Cautiously, I opened the living room door and stole a look at my father's motionless body. He was still asleep. Strange sounds punctuated his rhythmic breathing. The smell of cooking filled the house. I crept to the kitchen to eavesdrop on my mom and Kifah, who were whispering to each other.

"It's like I told you, she's pregnant. I swear, if I see that little Nus Nseis playing with them, I'll cut off her legs. Those bad boys will ruin our reputation."

IV

My father left at three in the morning.

But I only woke up at six, breakfast time, to the fragrant herbal maramiyya tea brewing.

My sisters and I laid out the round wooden tray, where my mother had put the teapot and pieces of stale bread for us to dip into the warm ful. I almost dozed off again, but the biting cold jolted me awake. We took turns washing our faces, fighting over who got the bathroom next. We put on our blue school uniforms with our little aprons and white woolen tights. Our mom braided our hair, fastening it with hairbands like she always did. She tied white satin ribbons in bows over the bands to hide them.

I heaved my bookbag on my back, grabbed a za'atar sandwich, and set off to meet Abdullah at the corner so we could walk to school together. My mother's distant voice chased after me, "Pay attention to your teacher and focus. Don't get into trouble!"

We got to school and walked in through the main gate. It was painted blue like the UNRWA flags that were fluttering high in the wind. We stood in neat, orderly lines waiting for the bell to ring and announce the beginning of morning classes. The best students were at the front, getting ready to present the morning bulletin after they'd raised the Palestinian flag. The bell rang, and our collective voice sang out the Palestinian national anthem:

> *Baladi,*
> *My land, the land of my ancestors,*
>
> *Fedayee,*
> *My people, an eternal people.*

The nickname Nus Nseis stuck to me at school because of my reputation for always managing to dodge fights. During the first semester, Abdullah and I were the leaders of a little clique that we'd formed.

I'd sit them down, our group of boys and girls, and tell them all about my adventures in the cactus grove. And they always listened, riveted. I taught them how to use the sheddeideh, the small slingshot that basically consisted of two pieces of wood tied together at the end by a sturdy piece of elastic. We used them to throw stones from a distance—either at the Israeli soldiers during demonstrations or at the birds in the grove when things were calm.

I spent a lot of my time telling the girls how good I was at riding bikes that were too big for me. I loved seeing the jealousy on their faces. I made a show of holding a magnifying glass toward the sun to channel its heat into burning some leaves. Everyone was impressed, everyone but Mona al-Astal, the math teacher's daughter. She always thought she was so much better than the rest of us just because her mom was a teacher, which meant the other teachers liked her and paid her more attention. They pampered her and treated her with such care. Only her.

The bell rang. It was time to go back to class. Mona hurried to take her spot in the front row, making sure that her desk was pushed right up against the teacher's.

Our teacher, Miss Zainab, entered the classroom. We all jumped up in unison to return her morning greeting, so vigorously that some floor tiles started to vibrate. They'd come loose from the sheer number of times they'd been scrubbed.

"Good morning, class."

"Good morning, Miss Zainab!"

She told us to sit back down. And we did. The room got very quiet very fast.

Miss Zainab scared me. We called her "Miss Z the Christian," because she wasn't Muslim like us. She was a large woman with short hair who wore skirts that barely covered her knees. Her thick-rimmed glasses made her eyes look smaller. She was cruel, like a nun in an orphanage, and she always dressed in black after her husband was martyred in the Intifada. She was angry about his death and took it out on us, the victims of her terrifying dictations:

"Yalla, write this down, *The rose is the very image of elegance.*"

She looked over Mona's shoulder at her notebook and ran her finger underneath the lines of writing, alerting her to a spelling error.

"Pay attention to the shape of the kind of 'ta' you are writing. They aren't the same!"

She passed through the rows of students to catch the cheaters. She grabbed them from their chairs and ordered them to go sit in front of the window, next to her desk, her favored punishment spot.

The bell rang and the period was over. She told us to lift our pens immediately, to not make even one more mark on our papers. She had Mona collect our notebooks and put them on her desk so she could correct them. Mona gladly obliged, then sat back down and opened her book to get ready for geography.

Geography class began. Miss Zainab asked us to show where Palestine was located.

Mona's hand shot up, as usual. She was frantically waving her finger around, irritating me to no end. So I started waving my own finger around to provoke her and Miss Zainab. But after waving it so hard, I felt a popping pain in my joints, and I realized it was all for nothing. I whispered to Rehana, the girl sitting next to me, "Just watch, she'll call on Mona and pretend she didn't see me."

I held up my arm with my other hand and started wagging my finger again. But sure enough, Miss Zainab picked Mona. "Once again, Mona's the only one who's done her homework!"

I was seething. I felt I would explode like a hand grenade and kill everyone in class. Miss Zainab and Mona first.

This wasn't the first time that Miss Zainab had paid special attention to Mona. Most teachers in refugee schools paid more attention to the daughters of other teachers and principals. As for us—the camp girls, the daughters of workers—we were treated no better than rats. During morning assemblies, they would line us up to get vaccinated against some disease or another, for fear of an outbreak that could spread among us and be transmitted to the citizens of Gaza.

We were treated differently. We were constantly reminded that we weren't from there, that even if we were hardworking, we didn't have the same rights.

I stopped competing with Mona. I decided instead to make myself relevant by giving the other students reasons to fear me, just like Nidal did in our neighborhood. I showed them how brave I was by stealing all the chalk so Miss Zainab couldn't find anything to write with. I even put worms in her handbag, promising my classmates that I'd take my revenge on her soon. And I always did everything I told them I would.

I concocted a plan to steal the new exam booklets from the cupboard at the back of the classroom and hand them out to the girls in our clique before Miss Zainab could give them to the teacher's daughters.

I sketched out the plan on a piece of paper and whispered to Rehana to hand it to Abdullah. But we got caught. Rehana got scared, started whimpering, and dropped the note on the ground. Just as I was about to pick it up, Miss Zainab slammed her long wooden ruler down on the desk. Everyone stopped reading and turned to see what was going on.

Miss Zainab stood up and walked over toward Rehana and me. I was terrified she'd get her hands on the note and see what I'd planned. I knew how angry she'd get: she'd send me to the principal's office to be punished in front of everyone at the next morning's assembly.

She was getting closer and closer. I was trying really hard to reach the paper with my foot and slide it toward me. I managed to get it. I swiftly leaned over and grabbed it. But she caught me.

"Give me that! Right now."

I ignored her. With a second swift motion, I stuffed it in my mouth and started chewing.

Miss Zainab lost it. Her steps heavy, she stomped over to my desk, pulling down her shirt to hide her sagging stomach as she walked. It was really tight on her. She ordered me to stand up and hold out my hands. She lifted the wooden ruler and brought it down hard on my palms, right to left and back again, not even stopping long enough for me to rub them on my uniform to ease the pain. As she beat me, I fixated on her bulging belly to distract myself. This helped me ignore the splinters that were lodging themselves beneath my skin. She was unrelenting, furious, hitting me on my back and thighs. It hurt, but I refused to shed a tear—and this only made her madder.

I managed to escape when the janitor entered the classroom to empty the wastebasket. She yelled at me to sit down, suddenly worried that the period was going to end before she'd taught us anything. I did as she said. Anger rose in my throat like molten lava, choking me, threatening to erupt. I was so angry I could barely breathe. I glared at her as she swayed heavily back to her desk. Right then and there, I decided I'd get my revenge.

At the end of the last period of the day, while she was absorbed in correcting our spelling tests, I quietly crept over and stole the classroom key from the edge of her desk. Luckily for me, she didn't suspect a thing. I locked her in that classroom and sprinted toward our little clique. They were waiting for me outside, in our school's dirt courtyard.

We all ran away, and I sang out gleefully, basking in my victorious revenge,

Like a barrel, she'll bulge and swell,
The bear goes over to the well,
She met the pig and down she fell,

Trapped inside, the cover shut,
Our Miss Zainab is a butt.

Prancing around with my friends, I belted out my own version of the nursery rhyme and led the way to Abu Mahmoud al-Kahtut's sweet shop. He would curse us every time he saw us through the window. I swiped some of the golden awwama that were neatly arranged in rows on giant aluminum trays to share with my friends.

Everyone went back to their houses, and I made my way toward the African Quarter.

I was feeling proud of myself for getting back at her. Not just for myself but for the other kids in our neighborhood too. The UNRWA schools discriminate against us. They can't even see us.

Evening fell and everyone peeled off one by one, leaving me to walk the rest of the way alone. Suddenly joy and victory gave way to fear. I feared my mother's switch and my grandfather's crutch. I was afraid of the black hose in the bathroom I knew she'd whip me with for coming home so late and for locking up the teacher.

Then I realized I was lost. I searched in the dark for the intersection that led back to our neighborhood.

I could already picture the red welts and bruises my father's leather belt would leave all over my body. I was sure my mother would tell him what had happened when he came home from work that weekend. But by then my story would already be the talk of the town. I felt a pit in my stomach at the possibility of our clique getting disbanded because the other children at school would no longer be allowed to play with me. And that Abdullah and Rami's mother would forbid them from talking to me. I walked along, wishing I'd get hit by a car and die on the spot.

Where we lived, even the smallest thing frightened us. We were afraid of dying, afraid of worms eating away at our flesh. Rumors instilled a fear in us that even the Israeli missiles couldn't, though we were well aware that these might fall from the sky at any moment and decimate us.

I thought about how Nidal would make fun of my dismal failure. The whole sky had gone dark. There was a chill in the air. I stumbled upon the way to the grove and breathed a sigh of relief when my surroundings started to look familiar because I definitely knew how to get to the house from there.

As I drew near the gate to the grove, I glimpsed a shadow slipping away into the subbar cacti. The dim yellowish lights of a car shone in my direction, right in my eyes. I realized I knew whose car it was. I recognized its distinctive rattle.

It was my father's friend, Saad al-Sarif. He owned an old white Volkswagen with a worn-out engine that clanked as he drove. Saad managed the local sewing factory, but on the side also sold used cars that he'd repaired to local people. The car pulled up next to me and stopped. I could see my mother's face through the window, the veins on her forehead nearly bursting with rage. She yanked open the door and charged over to me like a rampaging bull, grabbing my arm with one hand and fixing her headscarf with the other.

She dragged me into the car like a lamb to the slaughter. The harder she pulled, the more firmly I dug my heels into the ground. But I was no match for her. I burst into tears, "I swear I didn't do anything. She's the one who beat me. She's always picking on me because I hate Mona. I swear to God. Ask Abdullah. Ask Rehana. I didn't do anything."

She tugged me by the ear and threw me into the backseat.

In the car, silence. I thanked God that Saad al-Sarif had come with her to look for me. I figured that she wouldn't let him leave without inviting him in and offering him tea and snacks. They'd surely get to talking. And then she'd forget all about me getting lost and being late. I just wanted to go to sleep in peace. And not get hit anymore.

Things went exactly as I'd expected. Mom and Saad al-Sarif sat on our doorstep and talked about work and how his business was going.

I seized the opportunity to go to bed. I rested my head on the pillow, pulling the heavy quilt up over my face. I was exhausted and still wearing my dirty school uniform. No sooner had I drifted off than Amal's screams woke me. She ripped the covers off of me. "Hurry, get out of here! Mom's coming with the hose!"

My mother flailed at me like the witch in the Nus Nseis story, black hose in hand.

"You just watch how I'm going to whip the sense back into you! Who taught you to be such a tomboy?

You're out cavorting with boys, and you come back in the middle of the night! Where have you been, huh?"

I tried to take cover behind Kifah, but my mother's hose didn't know the difference between us. She thrashed us both. I was hopping around in place, crying. I wiped my nose on my school uniform and begged her to stop.

"Yamma, I swear to God I'm telling the truth. I wasn't with Rami or Abdullah. I didn't go to the grove. I got lost ... I was lost, I'm telling the truth. Don't hit me!"

The blows rained down on me like Israeli bullets falling on protesters in the refugee camps.

"I'm sorry, yamma! I swear I'm sorry!"

She threatened, "My God, just you wait until your father gets home. I'll let him kill you—no I'll kill you, just to be done with you and the shame you bring on us."

V

It was a short night for me.

I woke up to pain searing through my body. From the beating.

I could feel my eyes starting to swell. I was ashamed of the bruises that had started to show.

My mother sent me out to buy a dozen falafel. Standing in line, I noticed Abdullah asking for pickles and fried eggplant for his sandwich. I went over to where he was, but he shifted away from me. The boy at the shop wrapped my falafel in newspaper and I made my way back to the house. Everything in my body hurt so much that I begged my mother to let me stay in bed. I pretended to be sick, but it didn't work.

I got to school a few minutes late. I'd been waiting for Abdullah to come walk me to school, but he never showed up. I pushed open the blue gate and saw the orderly lines of students there, facing me, led by the school principal, Faiza.

The best students were standing up front, as usual,

ready to raise the flag and sing the national anthem. Everyone was staring at my swollen black eyes. Sweat pooling on my forehead, I stood there immobile. The principal ordered me to approach. She took my palm in her hand, opened it, and smacked it with a wooden ruler almost as long as the one my mother used when she sewed. She hit me right there in front of Miss Zainab, who glared at me with contempt. In front of Mona al-Astal, my archnemesis. In front of Abdullah, whose eyes flitted away every time I tried to meet his gaze. In front of all of them—the best students ... all the students.

This day had a decisive impact on my relationship with the group. The Palestinian flag was raised. My voice melted into all the others chanting our national anthem:

> *Vowing the oath beneath the shade of our flag*
> *For my land, my people, the fire of pain*
> *I will live a fedayee*
> *I will forever be a fedayee*
> *I will die a fedayee.*

I thanked God that Abdullah hadn't told my mom what happened and that the news didn't spread like I thought it would. The Israelis had imposed a curfew on the neighborhood and the workers in the Gaza Strip had called a new general strike: I'd been spared.

Al-Bilbeisi shut up shop early. Everyone in the neighborhood shuttered their windows and locked their doors, fearful of the green military jeeps prowling the dusty streets, threatening us through their loud-speakers: "Go home, go back home."

VI

The mood in the neighborhood grew really tense with the curfew and the strike. What made matters worse was that one of the fedayeen found the body of a girl in the grove where he'd been trying to hide among the subbar cacti to escape from the Israelis.

The discovery of the dead girl with the mutilated face was the talk of the neighborhood. Most people believed that occupation soldiers had slashed her face with a razor, raped her, killed her, and thrown her in the grove. But others thought that she might have been one of those girls with a reputation and was murdered by her family out of shame.

The whole thing was suspicious. It ripped through the neighborhood like a shockwave. Our mother no longer even let us out of her sight. I was cut off from Rami and Abdullah completely. They'd disappeared along with their own mother. The three of them had moved to the Jabalia refugee camp.

Time passed slowly. There was a general strike

and a curfew. We were forbidden from going out, so I started playing out back with my sisters. To kill time, my mother taught me how to sew. I worried about Rami and Abdullah. I wished someone would tell me how they were.

I spent most of my time studying for my end-of-year exams and competed with the neighborhood boys to prove who could stay up the latest. Through my window, I could still see the dim yellow of their faraway lights, spurring me on to keep revising. Things calmed down in the neighborhood after the Israelis lifted the night-time curfew and moved on to the next neighborhood. Everyone was relieved—life filtered back out onto the streets and our mother let us play in front of the house once again.

My first day back at school, I was so happy, fully prepared to take my exams. That day went well, except for passing rain showers. We got wet leaving school as we walked home in the early darkness of winter.

When I reached the intersection leading into the neighborhood, I could sense footsteps behind me. I panicked and didn't dare turn around. I picked up my pace but could feel the footsteps behind me get faster too. I tripped and fell flat on my face. My books and pens splattered out all around me on the wet street. Whoever it was behind me reached his hand out to help me up, whispering in my ear, "Don't be scared, I'm not going to hurt you."

I turned to the source of the sound, hands shaking in fear, tongue-tied, and paralyzed with terror. I stared at him, eyes agape—I couldn't believe what I was seeing. He was collecting my scattered things and returning them to my schoolbag. I couldn't make sense of anything. No one came outside to help me. Then I noticed that his shirt was streaked with blood. His dusty face was covered with a green keffiyeh, his eyes exhausted. Stuffing my things back into my bag, he informed me, "Tomorrow I'm heading for the crossing. I found work with some Jewish people and I'm not coming back. I wanted to say goodbye."

Then, like a ghost, his figure melted into the darkness of the neighborhood.

I struggled to stand up and shake the rain off my school uniform. I pulled it back down over my knees. I tried to pick the blood off my white woolen tights. They'd crusted onto my skinned knee. I hugged my soaking wet schoolbag close to me, wiping away the traces of blood and dust that he'd left on it. Limping, I dragged myself to the gate of our house. I pulled back the gray blanket and pulled myself together. I walked inside, flung my things in the hallway, and locked myself in the bathroom.

Luckily, my sisters had sealed the room up against the rain. I could hear the sewing machine rattling away in the living room as I darted into the other room. I turned on the hot water heater and rubbed the blood stains off my knees and books.

We all were awakened by the shrieks of Umm Riyala. She was slapping her cheeks in grief and bashing her head against our neighborhood's one tall electricity pole. She'd found the mutilated body of her son, Nidal, hanging from it.

Terrified by the shrieking, we rushed outside to see what was going on. We found his corpse swinging from the pole, the front of their house painted with the words, *This is what happens to spies.*

A green Israeli army jeep appeared at the intersection leading to our neighborhood, and our mother hurried us back inside. She closed the door and sealed the windows shut. We all crammed ourselves into the back room and sat in the darkness. Umm Riyala couldn't stop sobbing and wailing. The Israelis spoke through their loudspeaker: "Go inside your house. It is forbidden to go outside. Go inside. Go inside."

We were all horrified by what had happened. We didn't believe that Nidal could be collaborating with the Israelis.

Everyone on our side of the street thought that the Afro-Palestinians across the way might have had something to do with it—especially the Abu Samras. Nidal had fought with their eldest son. When Umm Riyala found out that he'd beaten up Nidal, she hung a severed donkey's leg in their doorway to frighten them. She'd also exacted her revenge by insisting that Abu Samra's martyred son not be buried in the martyr's cemetery. Racist, she also made it a point to say that because they were Black they were not welcome among us.

Before Nidal was killed, the antagonism between the Abu Riyalas and Abu Samras was the talk of the neighborhood. Everybody could hear them yelling at each other at all hours of the day and night.

Umm Riyala went a little crazy after that. She walked the silent streets cursing the Abu Samras and all of the Afro-Palestinians, blaming them for Nidal's murder.

"They killed my son. They mutilated him. They killed my son!"

The neighborhood became a scary place to live. My mother was convinced that the Israelis had a hand in this. Kidnappings and theft were on the rise. Israeli soldiers started barging into people's houses, bullets flying, as they searched for the fedayeen. We'd sometimes flee with our mother to our Abu Shanab grandparents' house to take cover.

Local people whispered that occupation soldiers were raping Palestinian girls so they could later recruit them as spies in exchange for not exposing their shameful secret. This gave my mother even more reason to worry about us girls, especially since my father had migrated to the Emirates to look for work. She was left to look after us alone.

VII

Our mother woke us up just before dawn. She ordered us to wash our faces. We were confused and complained as she combed our hair and got us ready to go.

She went about gathering our travel documents, birth certificates, and school records, stashing them all in the black Samsonite suitcase. She gave it to Kifah and told her to lock it. We didn't understand. We exchanged bewildered glances at the sight of the tears streaked with black kohl running down our mother's face.

She covered her charcoal black hair with a rose-patterned silk scarf. She checked that our cotton dresses were neat and tidy one last time and, noticing a little thread hanging between the pleats of Amal's dress, bit it off with her teeth.

I could hear the clanking of Saad al-Sarif's car pulling up to Grandpa Abu Diab's house. We said goodbye to Grandma Hadbaa and didn't even wait for our grandpa to come back from school. Mom stuffed us into the backseat and sat up front next to Saad, who started for the Egyptian border.

An Israeli soldier stopped us to check our identity papers and exit permits before Uncle Saad bade us farewell. Then we got into a taxi to take us to the other side of the border controlled by the occupation forces. We stopped to be photographed. The photographer covered his head with a black cloth and took a picture of us all. My mother clipped one to the top of the permit and saved the other one in her handbag.

We stood in a long line of travelers. People around us were speaking a mix of Arabic and Hebrew. Eventually, we boarded a big bus and my mother made us all sit with her. She reassured us and said that we were headed to the desert to live with our dad. She talked to us about how easy life was in the Gulf and told us stories of Palestinians who had moved there and never lacked for any comfort ever again.

I fixated on Surah Ya-Sin, the golden lettering stitched onto black cloth hanging from the rearview mirror. The bus driver had stuck some black-and-white photos on the window beside him: one of his brother in prison, the others of his children.

The Israeli soldier finished inspecting our papers and got off the bus. Sitting on my big sister's lap, I said goodbye to our country through the window. I cried because I was tired. Because I hadn't been able to say goodbye to Grandpa Abu Diab. Because I was going

to miss my crazy Grandma Hadbaa and our house ...
and Abdullah, who didn't even know about our sudden
departure.

VIII

We arrived in the village of Boumaiz in June 1986. My father was living in a little caravan with some Asian migrant workers. He'd found work there as a heavy vehicle driver of a water tanker, transporting clean drinking water to Emirati Bedouins who lived in the desert. When we got there, my mother started insisting on building a bedroom and a living room for us to stay in. It was hot, stiflingly hot, and we were locked inside all day helping our parents build these new rooms. We were only close with a few people, workers who had recently arrived there and were our only neighbors. They were mostly Asian, except one Sudanese man who lived next door. His job was to extend the power lines to the village where we all lived.

I spent entire days in that caravan with my sisters. Lying around on the carpet, desperate to feel less hot, we squirmed all over until we found the spot the air conditioner reached the best. My father left for work in the morning and came back in the afternoon at three.

My mother worked at home, cooking on the small gas canister she'd set up outside the caravan on the desert sand.

We helped her wash dishes and water the little palm tree growing next to the caravan. We didn't have enough money to buy dishwashing soap, so my mom used a mix of charcoal, vinegar, and wild green lemons to wash them with, wiping away fresh tears she always blamed on the onions she had chopped.

My mother took full advantage of the empty space in front of the rooms we'd finished constructing. She planted a henna tree and a lemon tree, as well as fragrant jasmine bushes. She also built a small chicken coop in the area out back, like the one my Grandma Amneh had back in the African Quarter. She started selling eggs and chickens to the workers and with the money bought a goat that we liked to play with.

Were it not for my mother, my father never would have been able to cope so far from other people out in this isolated desert.

She asked the laborers who worked irrigating the rich local people's farms to bring us vegetables in exchange for a home-cooked meal. Our favorite days were those when my father would bring a colleague home for lunch. We'd scamper to the bedroom like kittens, peeping at the visitor through the tiny crack in the door to amuse ourselves. My big sister Kifah had to rush off to the kitchen to help our mother make lunch and serve the tea and coffee.

We'd go outside to play with the goat my mom had bought, watching the stray camels and cows scavenge through piles of trash for food scraps. When we went out onto the dusty road near our house, we could see nothing but soft desert sand, little dunes to climb up and roll down, their heat searing through our bodies.

Sometimes we went to the goat pen right by where our Sudanese neighbor, the electrician, lived. We looked after them until he got home from work. We fed them our own leftovers and gave them whatever water was left in the tanker or truck my father was watering our trees with. Worried about us being outside around the male workers, our mother kept a watchful eye from behind the heavy curtains. When it was time to prepare tea for my father, we went home. We woke him up, always begging him to take us to one of the big cities about an hour away from the village. Every time, he protested that he didn't have a car, the water tanker only had two seats, and he'd be fired for using it to transport his family.

Sometimes we begged our neighbor to lend our father his company car, and my mother scolded us for having gone there without her knowledge. We'd also get yelled at for getting too near my father and waking him too early.

When it started getting late and our father still hadn't woken up, we went to sleep, anticipating the next morning's visit to the goat pen.

There was no way around boredom in Boumaiz except sleep.

Later we met the new Pakistani friend my dad had made, Akbar Khan. He'd just moved to the village with his wife. She taught us how to cook some tasty dishes like parathas and chai karak—a tea prepared with condensed milk, cardamom, and cinnamon. Akbar Khan's job was to slaughter sheep for Eid. We couldn't believe our eyes when he gave us a sheep on the first Eid al-Adha we celebrated in Boumaiz. He had stolen it from the estate of the rich khaleeji he worked for, having told his employer that one of his sheep died from the heat. Akbar Khan lived on the farm with these animals in the middle of the desert with no human or jinn to keep him company. My father regularly went to visit him and brought him food. Sometimes he took us with him too—to see the farm: the sheep, camels, goats, poultry, and various birds he watched over.

That day of Eid al-Adha, we awoke to the sounds of prayers from the Abu Shakur al-Battani mosque. We then started straightening up the bedroom, living room, and kitchen. We mopped all the floors. Our father had bought us matching colorful dresses from Naif Souq, a market frequented by Indians and Pakistanis because it was cheap.

We sat waiting at the door for my mother's family to show up. They lived in the big cities far away. But evening fell and brought no one with it. So to relieve our boredom and cheer us up, our mom asked us to help her wrap up the meat for our dad to take to the laborers who were without their families on the holiday. We brought out large aluminum trays and blue plastic bags and sat ourselves around her, our little heads covered with white cotton gauze. We dipped the palms of our right hands in the sheep's blood and made handprints on the front of the house to ward off evil. But the Eid came and went, and no one visited us. We went along with our dad to give the meat to the workers. We got some sweets and fresh dates in return.

We lived those first years in Boumaiz as outcasts from my mother's wealthy family. The only time any of them ever came to see us was if they needed a pit stop when traveling between cities to visit each other. And they'd only stop at our house long enough to relieve themselves, give their children a bite to eat, and get back on the road.

Before taking off, my elder auntie Zahana always left us some hand-me-downs. And without fail, my father always threw them into the iron trash barrel. My mother would cry and fight with him, every time.

"Let the girls have something new for once."

"I will not clothe my children in humiliation."

In late 1988, my father lost his job. That morning, we woke up to the sound of him and my mother arguing. She was criticizing him for quitting the job her brother had given him.

"Your laziness is going to ruin us. Just be patient, he'll pay you."

"Your family are all cheats, frauds, and swindlers!"

My mother started packing up her things into the suitcase that she'd stowed atop the wooden wardrobe, the one that was not to be used until our return to Gaza. She walked out of the room with us trailing at her feet, crying as she yelled, "I won't live with a failure! You're so lazy—everyone else is successful. Everyone but us!"

But my father took not being paid at work as a personal affront—not only to him, but to his wife and daughters too. He already thought it was insulting to have deigned to work for that farmer, Abu Shanab's son. The known cheat.

My mother sat on her big brown leather suitcase right out there in the middle of the desert. She kept wiping the sweat off her face, and if we tried to approach her, she rebuked us:

"Go inside or I swear I'll kill you one by one. I can't stand the lot of you."

So my sisters and I went into the bedroom to keep an eye on her from behind the heavy curtain. We watched our father go out and attempt to convince her to come back in. But she refused every time, and their argument kept escalating.

I saw that he was heading for the bedroom, so I alerted my sisters:

"Turn out the light, quick. Hurry up! Dad is back and he's angry."

We lay on the floor, clinging to each other. The room was silent as the grave. Our father angrily yanked the blanket from our faces. The ash of his Lucky Strike fell into my mouth. I gulped, repulsed. He went on smoking.

"You, get up. You, too. Go make some bread. And get lunch ready. The bitch doesn't want to come back into the house."

Kifah jumped up in a panic, and we hurried behind her to start kneading the dough and making the coffee to dampen his rage. Amal and I quietly slipped out to look for our mom and bring her back. I spat out the cigarette ash. The desert sand burned our bare feet. We spotted her from afar. She was sitting in front of Muhammad al-Bengali's shop, a plastic water bottle in hand.

When he was unemployed, my dad was always home. Then the fighting between him and my mom got worse. Our daily routine was punctuated by them sniping at each other.

"I rue the day I agreed to marry you. I'd have been better off with someone from the back alleys than the likes of you!"

"You should be grateful, farmer girl. You, your dad, your peasant family, you think you're good enough for Bedouin shaykhs?"

"Right, like we really want to marry lazy bums living in tents with faces eaten by fleas."

"It's better than being a traitor! If your dad wasn't a collaborator, the Israelis would never have let him become mukhtar. You're disgusting, all of you."

My father followed my mother out of the house. She threatened to slash open his stomach with a kitchen knife. He left her outside, locked the door, and went to bed. After he fell into a deep sleep, we opened the door for her, and she spent the night with us in our room.

My father slept all day and only rose at dawn to wake my mother so she could prepare his food. She refused and scolded him if he woke us up early too. So he opened a tin of sardines and ate that.

The days he spent at home, out of work, felt like some sort of hellish jail. He kept inventing excuses to hit and kick us and spit in our mother's face. He was looking for any outlet for his anger.

He turned on the little TV to watch the news. He was closely monitoring all the developments of the Intifada and followed every detail. He turned up the volume whenever they played revolutionary songs, drowning out the sound of the air conditioner.

In the colors of Palestine he is shrouded
he is shrouded in green,
he is shrouded in red,
he is shrouded in white,
he is shrouded in black.

We stopped talking so as not to annoy him. Otherwise we'd bear the brunt of his anger and hear those usual curses, *You and her—go to your room, damn you. Go inside! I don't want to hear another peep out of you.*

Observing him from behind the door, we could tell that he was living that moment as if he were the one throwing stones and getting shot at. The Children's Revolt of the First Intifada had broken out. He inspected every face on the screen, trying to see if he could recognize anyone. He wanted to feel like he'd never left Gaza, that he hadn't missed out on anything.

He was glued to the screen, watching a video of Israeli soldiers breaking the bones of a seventeen-year-old with rocks. Amal pinched me and ran off. I got up to chase her, only for my head to bump into my father's belly. He hit me, kicked me, cursed me:

"I swear to God, I'll mop the floor with your blood, you little bitch. What did I tell you all, huh?"

I wriggled free of him with great difficulty and escaped to the chicken coop to hide. Amal was close behind and stuck her tongue out at me.

My father called out to my mother, "Hind, come here, quick. They got Abu Kirsh's son. They broke his bones."

My mother rushed over to the television, terrified, to see for herself.

"Poor Umm Rami, poor woman. They killed her son. God give her strength and the patience to endure. May He break all their bones in return."

She covered her head with her white prayer shawl and went over to our neighbor Akbar Khan's house. She wanted to use their telephone to call the international central exchange. But she collided with me as I was trying to get away from the crazy red chicken that was fluttering after me and pecking at me, thinking I was trying to steal her eggs. Amal was right behind me, still making fun of me. My mother pushed me over the doorstep and gave me a scolding.

"Go inside. What are you doing still out in this heat? Go in or you'll get heatstroke."

But I followed her to the neighbors' to find out what was going on. She only used their phone if there was an emergency. I overheard what she said to her father—I heard her say Rami's name. I froze. I was suddenly so afraid for Rami and Abdullah that the tears flowed uncontrollably from my eyes. Memories of our neighborhood, the grove, that masked-up face with a keffiyeh wrapped around it surfaced all at once. Could Rami have gone back to Gaza ... had occupation soldiers caught him? Had they killed him? I couldn't speak. I let my mother tell our neighbor what had happened. I ran off behind the house and climbed the iron ladder up to the roof. By then I was sobbing, caught up in the past, seized by the terror that Abdullah might have been martyred now that they'd captured his brother.

The red chicken still had an eye on me. She was scratching the desert sand with her beak. Throwing stones at her from the roof, I yelled, "What are you looking at you bitch?!"

I climbed back down and splashed some water from the big white plastic tank on my face. I headed to the bedroom to bury myself under a bedsheet so my sisters wouldn't notice my red-rimmed eyes and make fun of me. My mother came in a few minutes later and ripped off her prayer shawl, the heat unbearable. It fell to the ground. She slammed the door behind her so forcefully that our Jamal al-Mahamel print fell off the wall. The nail it was hanging on fell too. My father picked up the nail and started hammering it back in with his sandal. He hung the print on its nail and turned up the TV.

Where are the masses?
Where are all the Arabs?
Where? Where?

My mother sat beside him and shared the bad news she'd heard from her father about the Intifada and how scary things were getting in the neighborhood.

I lay in the bedroom, eyes closed, hoping that God would answer my prayers. I wanted to go back to our neighborhood immediately. I needed to check on Rami and Abdullah.

My mother called me and my sisters to help her pick the freshly washed and dried cotton out of the cushions. We finished picking out the cotton and Kifah sewed new pillows out of it.

The television went quiet. My father turned out the lights in the living room and lay down on the mattress on the floor. My mother tossed him a new pillow to sleep on.

IX

In a rare turn of events, my prayers were answered.

The phone rang at our Sudanese neighbor's house. He rushed over to wake my father. Until then it had just been like any other boring Friday. But then Amal opened the door for our neighbor, who'd been outside pounding away persistently. My father came back in, wringing his hands in worry. He'd just gotten the news that his father, Grandpa Abu Diab, had been taken ill.

He kicked at the paving tile that Sabreen and I had been playing with, using it as a makeshift tray to serve tea on. His anger was pulsing through the wrinkles on his face, and we sensed he was about to erupt. We fled to the bedroom.

He made the decision to travel on the spot. He was conscious that living far from home might deprive him of his final farewell. The next day at dawn, we all stuffed ourselves into our old Buick Roadmaster. Squeezed tightly between my sisters in the backseat, I struggled to get a bit more comfortable and at least stretch out my legs.

We pressed our faces up against the rear window, routinely pushing away the short velvet curtain covering it so we could see outside. But the sun beat down on us so strongly that we inevitably pulled the curtain closed as soon as we'd opened it. To make matters worse, the air conditioner was so weak it didn't even reach us in the backseat. I cursed my older sisters, who always got the comfortable seats up front. Silently we slept, without complaint. Whining was strictly forbidden. We knew that even one peep out of us and we'd be punished by a beating from our father.

My mother sat next to him up in the front seat, chatting away about neighborhood gossip. She relayed everything she'd been hearing from her father. To keep himself alert and occupied, my father turned up the radio to listen to the news. Every now and then he'd call out to my mother, "Hind … Hind, you're not asleep, are you?" Jolted back to consciousness, my mom would say, "No, of course not! I'm awake." When we reached the land border with Saudi Arabia, it was four in the morning.

I was excited to cross over into the sands of a different desert. Everything was quiet. I let my mind wander, secretly rejoicing that I'd be meeting Abdullah and Rami again soon. We'd been gone a while and we'd just suddenly packed up and left without saying goodbye. I was already coming up with the excuses I would have to use to wriggle away from my mother to slip out and meet them at the grove like I used to.

When we arrived, my father would be so busy with visitors that my absence from my grandpa's house wouldn't be noticed. The idea comforted me. I was sure that when we got back to the African Quarter, all the neighbors would come to see my father and check in on my grandpa. Everyone would come—cousins, distant relatives, neighbors of neighbors, maybe even friends who lived far away.

They'd celebrate his return after such a long absence. Surely some people would show up greedy for gifts, and maybe others with hopes of picking one of us to be their future wife once we'd more or less grown up. As we sped through the darkness, an amber glow shone down on my face each time we passed under one of the enormous streetlights. My mind was racing. I dozed on and off, my legs tangled with those of my sisters.

I tried to kill time counting the streetlamps, one by one.

My little sister Sabreen wiggled and kicked me, so I kicked her in the stomach to get her back. Annoyed, she squealed, "You idiot, stop banging into me. What am I supposed to do? Where do you think I can go?" Alerted to the shrieking coming from the backseat, my father made a threat that was really more of a promise, "Enough! If you don't shut up, the lot of you, I'll throw you out into the desert and leave you and all my troubles behind."

We were terrorized and immediately went silent. We fell back asleep afraid of rousing his anger.

We woke up when my father turned off the engine. Morning had broken. Kifah opened the back door. "Yalla, get out. Dad wants to rest for a couple of hours."

My father had stopped at a large white mosque topped by a gold-trimmed green dome. He went in to the men's side to nap. We also needed to rest, so we went over to the women's side with our mom. He asked them to bring us a big plate of biryani.

Dad then carried on driving after my mom had poured him tea out of the thermos that she always kept beside her. On the fourth day of our endless journey, we finally reached Russeifa, in Jordan. My father claimed to have family there.

My mom wasn't a fan of this idea. She feared that my dad might have secretly planned to marry one of us off to some Bedouin relative of his and we'd end up like her.

"Where are you planning to put them all? They're young ladies now, how can they just sleep over in this house with people we don't even know?"

"What are you talking about? It's my family. Stop nagging at me."

"Your family? The Qatatwas? Where are your people even from? They're rootless, they have no lineage. You're scattered all across the Sinai."

"Shut up. Don't shame us. Someone might hear you."

Somaya Qatawi's loud welcomes stopped my parents from fighting. My mom went silent immediately. She started bustling us out of the car, unloading our little bags that held a change of clothes for each of us.

We got out and went into Somaya's house. She greeted us warmly. "Welcome, we're so happy you are here. Mashallah, look at these beautiful young ladies. Come in, you're welcome here, auntie. Come in and sit inside with my daughter Taghreed."

We followed Taghreed into the bedroom. Mom stayed with dad, Somaya, her husband, and their five sons outside in the yard. Somaya's husband Tawfiq lit a kerosene lamp so they could see better.

Outside in the courtyard, they'd planted a lemon tree and a little orange tree. Bountiful jasmine vines covered the wall surrounding the house. Their perfume wafted on the cool dawn breeze.

We all sat on a mattress on the ground. My mother bristled at both the mattress and its cloth cover, comparing them to our beds back in Boumaiz. They were visibly stained. She made no effort to hide her revulsion.

"She's so disgusting—her and her house and her cups that smell of eggs. You Bedouin are seriously disgusting. You're like animals, you'll never be human."

My mom refused to drink tea out of the glass they offered her. She'd spotted tiny cockroaches scurrying around the copper serving tray. She pretended to be suffering from heartburn. When Somaya's husband, Tawfiq, went to the kitchen to get the huge tray of mansaf he'd prepared, she followed. My mom seized the opportunity to whisper in my dad's ear, "She's filthy. Her whole house is filthy. Look at her cups—they stink!

You people are disgusting, I'm serious. You'll always be Bedouins. You'll never be civilized."

My mom knew that this grand reception, and the visit itself, wasn't because of the Qatatwas' generosity. Or because they were gracious hosts. There was an ulterior motive. She could see right into my father's mind. He was concocting a plan to get close to his Bedouin family, as he needed support after failing to produce a male heir. Now that his own father was approaching death, he felt this more acutely. There was no one left to carry on the family name. No one but his relatives living inside the occupied territories—the ones who'd remained on their lands and hadn't left during the Nakba. But how could he communicate with them, let alone see them, after being displaced as a refugee, barred from entering his father's land?

We all huddled around the mansaf. Somaya brought out yogurt, traditional Palestinian salad, and fresh green peppers. Everyone ate except my mother. She made a show of being busy with us, fussing and feeding us. Somaya stared straight at us the whole time, at our faces, our bodies. She looked each of us up and down, one by one, and studied the way we ate, sat, laughed, and even how we blushed.

Our mom was inspecting Somaya to further confirm her suspicions. She lost it when Somaya suggested to my dad that we should spend the night and leave the next morning. She clamped her hand down over his, shooting him an indignant look. Met with his silence, she exploded, "Where do you want your daughters to sleep? In this hole? With all these boys around? Go on, get up. It's only a few more hours to your father's house. We can all sleep more comfortably there."

Mom asked Somaya if we could use their bathroom to shower, wash our hair, and change into our spare dresses before stuffing ourselves back in the car. Somaya turned on the hot water heater and we all showered. We thanked her, said goodbye, and were crammed back into the car like sheep on Eid.

Dad got us to the border that the occupation forces had constructed in the Shuna area, separating Jordan and Palestine. He parked the car and left it there. We got in one of the taxis that took people across the border. Then we walked to the checkpoint. We waited for hours and got eaten alive by flies.

We sat on the ground next to our mom. Dad kept pacing back and forth inside the closed area, trying to eavesdrop on the Israeli soldiers. He pretended he didn't understand Hebrew. But every now and then he explained what was happening to my mother.

Sitting there with our mom, our exhaustion and anxiety visible on our faces, we spread out on the cool tiles and waited for the Israeli soldier to grant us permission to enter. We were surrounded by other travelers. A baby was crying. His mother was trying to calm him down but it wasn't working. Her husband shouted at her to quiet him, but this only made the infant cry louder. Then the mother started sobbing too, over the baby's tears. Our turn came. The soldier called out my father's name in Arabic:

"Fazaa Harb."

Dad rushed up to him, mom right behind him.

"You cannot cross. You don't have a birth certificate for the youngest girl."

My mother interrupted. "That's what we are here to do now, we're trying to add her name to her father's identity card. Here's her name. Look, it's on the UNRWA card issued by the UN."

The soldier didn't seem to be paying much attention. He looked over the UNRWA card and found Amal's name but not Sabreen's.

"Hajjeh, there's no other name here. Where is it?"

"She's a twin, this is her sister. Her sister's name is on the card, look here. You want to let her twin sister in and not her?"

"They're twins?"

"Yes, twins. The people in the Gulf made a mistake on the document. They didn't record her name, only her twin sister's. You know how those Gulf people are—they barely know how to read and write."

"What do you mean twins? One's so short, the other is tall."

"How can you question what God created? Look—you're tall, and that other soldier is short. This one came out little, like her dad."

"I see. Stay here, I'll check with the officer."

My dad looked at my mom, stunned by her fearless,

elaborate deception of the soldier. The way she'd shouted and scolded him, you'd think she was telling the truth. Even she was surprised at what had come out of her mouth. It was almost as if she'd been rehearsing for this moment. The Israeli soldier came back with two more officers from the occupying army. My mother burst into tears, certain that she'd been caught and that they'd come to arrest her for her lie.

One of the officers spoke. His voice was terrifying.

"Why are you crying?"

He spoke Arabic like a local.

"It's just too much. The way the Jordanian guards treated us at the border. The flies eating us alive. We couldn't get the filth out of our eyes. Everything stank. At least here you have clean chairs to sit on."

The officer stared fixedly at her. He spoke into the wireless device strapped to his shoulder.

Seeing our mother sobbing like that, we started crying too. Whenever she broke down, we always broke down with her. My father looked on, incredulous.

The other Israeli officer came up to us and, speaking to Kifah, asked if what our mother was saying was true. She didn't waver and replied immediately, "Yes, twins. I swear to God they're twins. One takes after our mother's side, the other our father's."

The two officers walked off. They came back five hours later.

We curled up around my mother to sleep. My father was trying to pick up on what the Israeli soldiers were saying. He was hoping for something reassuring to put our minds at rest. My mother refused to budge. She rejected my father's suggestion to go back to Somaya Qatawi's house, spend the night, and try to cross again in the morning.

"I swear to God, tonight I won't sleep until we get to Gaza."

"For God's sake, woman, you know you can't win against these people!"

"Leave me alone. You want to go, go. I'm staying here with my daughters."

She remained seated on the ground, with us spilling out of her lap. When it got to border closing time, my father rushed over.

"Come on, get up. I heard them talking about us, it's our turn."

She bolted upright and started smoothing out our dresses, whispering to us in a barely audible voice, "Don't be scared if they separate you. Whatever they ask, just say that Amal and Sabreen are twins. Not a word more. If they keep insisting and you get scared, make a scene."

We did exactly as my mother instructed. She actually succeeded in convincing the officer that Amal—who was a full three years older than Sabreen—was her twin sister.

They believed my mother. She kept her face serious and unsmiling the whole time so they wouldn't catch her in her lie. She knew that she would remain under strict surveillance until we were far away, back at our house in the African Quarter.

But she did steal a look at my father with victory in her eyes to remind him how resourceful she was, that she was always right to keep fearlessly pushing until she got what she wanted.

After the interrogation, we piled back onto our mother's lap, our eyes bloodshot, swollen nostrils still dripping. Even after so much effort, Sabreen almost gave it all away as the Israeli soldier was still surveilling us. My mother slapped her across the face. "You got your new dress all dirty. I swear I'm going to kill you."

Sabreen didn't understand and burst into tears, irritating the soldier. He ordered us into the inspection area to get rid of us. He escorted us to the crowded queue of travelers and left, returning to the waiting room outside.

We waited in line along with a throng of other travelers who were standing there and waiting, just like us, for the Israeli soldiers to call out their names to be searched.

Finally our turn came. One at a time, they ordered us to look into a black-tinted window. We couldn't see them, but they could see us.

An unknown voice called my father's name from behind the window. He responded by handing his papers to a soldier, who in turn handed them on to the person in charge, also behind the window. We walked up, one at a time, in the order that we were registered on my father's identity documents. Then they called my mother's name, Hind Abu Shanab. She had insisted on keeping her own name instead of changing it to her husband's. We saw many displaced people around us crying, their entry permits refused. We watched others be deported after being deemed a security threat. They lost their right of return to Palestine forever. They bade their families farewell for the last time. One woman gave us a bag full of gifts to take to her family in the Khan Yunis camp after they'd denied her permission to cross the border. Her permit had expired, and they refused to renew it.

Finally, we went into two separate rooms—one for men and one for women. They did a full body search on us. In the luggage inspection area, they opened and rifled through our big leather suitcases.

The female soldier started pulling apart the pillowcases that my mother had stuffed with clothes and the sheets she was going to use to decorate our house in Gaza. Another one ordered my mother to come alone into the room, where they did the full body strip searches. She told her to undress completely, ignoring my mother's pleas to let her keep on her underwear because she had her period.

We waited for my mother in the luggage area. While we were there, we witnessed a blonde Israeli soldier lift a bra and something black and lacy over her head, laughing cruelly at a young male traveler standing in front of her. He bowed his head in shame as she mocked him in broken Arabic, "So you wear women's lingerie?"

This made another soldier, who was right beside her, laugh as he sprayed himself with perfume he'd lifted from a suitcase he was inspecting. The man was frozen in place. He avoided her gaze and tried very hard not to look at anyone else in the room. He mustered up a shy response, "I bought that in Amman for my fiancée. I'm here to get married."

After we'd passed through all the steps of the search process and our bags and bodies were inspected, we rejoined our parents on the other side of the border. We all got on the bus waiting to take us into occupied Palestine.

They left us there to wait on that bus for an hour with the windows closed. An Israeli soldier boarded and demanded to see our identity papers and permits to enter Gaza. Then he got off.

The bus finally started to move. Our torture ended when the soldier lifted the iron barrier, allowing the bus to cross into Gaza.

Eventually, we got off the bus and into a Palestinian border taxi that would take us to Grandpa Abu Diab's house in the African Quarter.

When we arrived at our house, we yanked open the taxi door and ran up to the iron gate. We banged on it to announce our arrival, and Grandpa came outside to greet us, hugging us and smothering us with kisses. The driver helped my father carry the stuffed pillowcases and leather suitcases to the doorstep.

I brushed away my tears and hugged my grandpa tight. Then I immediately rushed in to check on my Grandma Hadbaa. She smacked me with her cane, thinking I was a thief, come to steal her cigarette. The brazier was lit, and its smell filled the room. She was sitting there in her Bedouin thobe, hand-stitched with blue thread. When she heard my father's voice, she pulled a scarf over her head and called out, "Fazaa, Harb, Fazaa, Harb, where are you? We're here."

My grandfather rang out in response, "Yes, we're here on the border with Gaza now. Tomorrow, I'll take you to see your family. Fazaa's girls are here with you."

My grandma wasn't aware of our existence. Grandpa said she'd lost her mind after becoming a refugee in 1948. He'd taken her all over the country and even to Egypt to find a cure, but nothing had worked.

Anticipating the arrival of new guests, Mom immediately started putting the house in order and mopping the floors. Dad lay down on the mattress on the floor and fell dead asleep. I seized my opportunity and slipped out to al-Bilbeisi's shop, ignoring how tired I was. I was hoping he'd tell me something about Rami and Abdullah. But he wasn't there. I found his son instead. Muhammad was a pharmacist studying in Egypt and had only come back to help his father in the shop for the summer. I asked him for an ice cream, a sandwich, and a bottle of 7-Up.

"If you bring back the bottle, I'll give you back a shekel."

"OK, I'll bring it back then, thanks."

On my way back home, I spotted Hassan, Abu Riyala's son—Nidal's younger brother. He was a young man now. He said hello, and I ran off toward the house. He was still following me, so I shouted at him:

"What is it? What's wrong? Why are you following me?"

"Tell your mother that my mom wants to come visit you this afternoon."

"Alright."

I relayed the message to my mother. But I had to wait a long time for my father to wake up before we could receive Umm Riyala. When she came, I stayed in the room with them, not because I liked Umm Riyala—I didn't—but because I was waiting for the slightest mention of Rami and Abdullah. My mother scolded me for sitting in the room with the grown-ups, so I left, but I kept making up excuses to go back into the room, like serving tea and coffee. Hours passed and still no mention of Rami or Abdullah. Instead of talking about what was happening in the neighborhood, she started talking about Nidal.

She looked right at me and started sobbing. She kept repeating how seeing me had brought back memories of him and how she wished he were still alive so she could marry me to him. She complained to my mother about Abu Riyala, who had taken a second wife, an Afro-Palestinian woman from the neighborhood. Apparently he'd started insulting Umm Riyala constantly, calling her crazy, saying that she'd lost her mind. She moved on from this to the Abu Samra family. She claimed they were the reason her family was destroyed. They were the reason her son was killed. She rambled on and on, even as other guests came to visit my parents. The house filled up with people welcoming us back and checking in on my grandparents. Yet none of them mentioned a thing about my two friends.

At one point, Hassan escorted me back to the shop so I could return my 7-Up bottle. I also had to buy nuts for the guests. Muhammad al-Bilbeisi returned my shekel. I used it to buy Tarboosh, chocolate-covered marshmallows on top of a thin biscuit layer. I bought one for each of us and the nuts for my mom. As we made our way back to the house, I felt a heavy grip on my right elbow and sensed a hand grabbing Hassan by his shirt collar. I turned my head. It was two Israeli soldiers, automatic weapons slung over their shoulders by a black strap. They were holding a can of red paint and two large paint brushes. They dragged us over to Abu Ayman's wall that overlooked the main road. One of the soldiers said in broken Arabic, "Yalla, paint here over the writing."

I was petrified. I saw the fear etched into the features of Hassan's face as he stood there, visibly shaking. The chocolates fell from our hands, and we lost the bag of nuts somewhere between our house and Abu Ayman's. Each of us grabbed a paintbrush, dipped it in the small can, and painted over the revolutionary slogans written on the abandoned wall. The messages called for people to go on general strike on Friday. They called for a Day of Rage in the Jabalia camp to protest the occupation.

I didn't have time to process what was going on. I'd been plucked out of my life into a nightmare. Revolutionaries, soldiers, and people throwing stones flashed through my mind. I'd witnessed these scenes on TV with my dad back in Boumaiz. It felt like I'd never left the neighborhood. Whatever fear I'd had of the occupation didn't come close to what I was feeling now. It was real: two Israeli soldiers, two guns pointed at our backs, mine and Hassan's. I wished my father or mother would step outside even for a second and save us. But that didn't happen. Seconds ticked by like an eternity.

I saw sweat dripping off Hassan's forehead. His pants were wet. He was painting the wall, hand shaky. I painted alongside him in total silence. We only turned around when we finished, but the two soldiers had already left. So we ran off. My dress was spattered with red paint. Hassan fled to his house, and I lost sight of him. I looked around for the bag of nuts, which I found in the same spot where I must have dropped it, covered in dirt. I shook it off and headed back. All I could think was how brave Rami had been to have withstood the soldiers breaking his bones with large rocks. Trembling, I went into the kitchen and divided the nuts into fancy serving bowls. Amal took them to offer to the guests. I hid out behind the house to get away from the commotion of the visitors and their loud voices. I needed quiet to think about what had just happened.

X

It had been five days since we'd arrived at Grandpa Abu Diab's, yet the neighbors were still dropping in. And since my mother was busy hosting them, she made Sabreen and I go help out my Abu Shanab grandparents at their large house. We'd get there first thing in the morning, and by the time we left in the afternoon, we were wiped out. People sometimes came to visit Grandpa Abu Shanab, seeking him out for various kinds of advice. He'd tell me off if he ever caught me talking to the boys who'd come along with their parents.

Grandma's list of chores never ended: wash the laundry, do the dishes, mop the floors. Unfortunately for us, she was obsessively clean. Sometimes she'd start talking about what she went through, how much she suffered after being displaced. She told us how she'd had to live in tents provided by the Agency. Then she went silent, every time. She reminded us how she'd given birth to our uncle Hashem at the border. After they'd been expelled from their village, Bayt Jirja, she'd walked the whole way, a few paces behind my grand-father, fleeing murder and destruction. She recounted the details of how she'd been forced to tear the hem of her thobe to clean the blood off her newborn baby and how she'd then used that same fabric to wrap him in so she could hold him in her arms and nurse him.

When he first arrived in the African Quarter, Grandpa Abu Shanab was able to build a house because he'd been chosen to act as the neighborhood mukhtar. People appreciated the skill and wisdom he had in helping them deal with complex issues. Within a few years, he'd con-verted the house into a small two-story building. He and Grandma lived on the ground floor. He'd also been able to recreate the beautiful garden he'd once had in Bayt Jirja, transforming the house into his own little paradise. He spent most of his time growing green peppers, tomatoes, cucumbers, and the sour green grapes whose vines hung down over the sitting area outside. Grandpa also grew spring onions and wild Damask roses, which perfumed the whole neighborhood.

What my racist grandma could never quite get over was how close her new house was to the street that sep-arated her from the Afro-Palestinian people across the way. She was convinced that someday the neighbors might scale the wall around the house to steal the eggs from her chicken coop. When she found out that they'd taken the lemons that had fallen onto the street from a branch of her tree that drooped over the wall, she cut that branch off.

We never finished our chores before five in the evening. And she wouldn't let us leave until she'd actually sniffed the tiled floors to check they were spotless and smelled fresh. She'd also go inside the kitchen and run her fingers over the dishes, checking for any traces of the lemon-scented dish soap. She even had a specific sponge for pots and another for glass juice cups, and she could tell if we'd used the wrong one. After she'd completed her cleanliness checks and deemed our work satisfactory, she'd then rummage through our clothes for anything stolen that we might have stashed away in the pockets of our dresses. It always felt like a curse to be the one chosen to stay overnight since it meant getting up at the crack of dawn to lug empty bottles to Abu Mansour's farm and fill them with fresh milk. It was just my luck, and no surprise considering my general misfortune, that this time it was my turn. My sisters teased me and happily left me there to stew in my resentment. I stayed on at Grandma's house, basking in my bad luck.

Grandma Amneh was up by four in the morning. She tuned the radio to the Voice of the Qur'an broadcast from Cairo. She made her wudu' and prayed. When I heard the clinking of empty milk bottles getting closer and closer to the room where I slept, I yanked the covers over my head so she'd leave me be. But sure enough, Grandma turned the door handle, marched in, and stripped the covers from my face and body. "Still asleep at this hour? Get up, it's late! Come on, go fill up these bottles and bring your grandfather his milk."

I got up. Rubbing my eyes, I struggled to drag myself over to the washbasin outside behind the house. I splashed cold water on my face. I collected the empty bottles and headed out through the iron gate at the back. I fumbled through the darkness, afraid that I might be stopped by an Israeli soldier who would arrest me—or beat me up and break my bones like they'd done to Rami. I picked up my pace so I could get to Abu Mansour's quicker. I pushed open his green iron gate with my free hand and walked through. There was already a line of women there, all waiting for Abu Mansour, who was still out milking the cows. When I got a little closer, I could make out Umm Riyala speaking to a young man. I said good morning. She was surprised to see me there so early; it was not yet daybreak. She grabbed my hand, "Really? You don't want to say hi to Rami? I'd thought you two were friends."

I was so surprised that it took a minute for me to process what she was saying. It felt like maybe I was dreaming. I looked up shyly at the young man. I never would have recognized him. He'd grown a long beard that covered his face and hid his dimples. He simply didn't look like the same person he was the last time I saw him. The milk bottles clanged against each other as I shifted them from right to left so I could shake his hand. As I extended mine, he immediately pulled his back, raising it to his chest and apologizing. "Sorry, I've just made wudu'. But welcome back to the neighborhood. Pass on my greetings to your parents."

He flung those words at me and just walked off with his full milk bottles. Once he was out of earshot, Umm Riyala reassured me, "Don't take it to heart, honey. After the occupation soldiers broke his arm, he no longer shakes hands with women. Now he's religious and keeps away from the rest of us."

I never expected to see such sorrow etched on Rami's face. It made me sad to see him like this. That handsome boy who liked to show off his newest jeans every chance he got was now wearing a long beard and a short jellabiya. The boy I once knew had died—the one who taught me to ride a bicycle, the one I'd spent my childhood hanging out with in the cactus grove. I went back to my grandparents', ruminating over what I'd seen, shifting the now full bottles of milk between my hands to give each a little rest as I walked along. Back at the house, I pried the gate open with my foot, handed my grandma the bottles, and helped her get breakfast ready.

XI

Grandpa Abu Shanab, sitting in the living room, adjusted the radio dial to tune into the BBC Arabic service. He turned up the sound. He sipped the coffee my grandma had made him. At seven o'clock on the dot, visitors started knocking at the door. People used to come from all over the Gaza Strip to seek his advice. In return, they would bring him offerings—a pound of sugar or toffee if they were poor, a box of McIntosh chocolates or a round blue tin of Danish butter cookies if they were better off. Grandma Amneh used to hide these expensive treats in her bedroom, stashed in a large leather suitcase that she'd stowed away safely atop her wardrobe.

I'd promised my sisters that I'd get my hands on some chocolate. So I ventured in while Grandma was busy with her guests. I climbed up on the side of her bed and tugged the end of the suitcase toward me. I managed to unzip it and started fishing around inside for the chocolate. My fingertips brushed against the paper wrapper of a box. I tore a piece off, burrowed my finger inside, and eased out as many chocolates as I could. This process was rather complicated: all the while, I had to keep an ear out for Grandma's footsteps. I knew that if she came too close I had to run away to avoid being caught in the act. I stuffed my pockets and pushed the suitcase back in place. I quickly shuffled out of the bedroom and made for the front door before she could get her hands on me. But she grabbed me by the collar of my dress before I could save myself and pinched my ear.

"Where do you think you're going, young lady? I didn't say you were done."

"No, Grandma, I wasn't leaving. I was just closing the gate so the neighbors can't get in."

"Fine. Go and get some eggs from the chicken coop. You can put them in the straw basket."

She hadn't searched me—what a relief. I headed over to the chicken coop reluctantly. I nudged the hens with my foot, stirring up dust from under them, hoping to strike gold—and steal it. I tucked two eggs away in my dress pocket and laid the rest in the little straw basket. I carefully placed the basket on her doorstep and made my escape before Grandma could get another chance to search me.

By the time I got back to Grandpa Abu Diab's house, my stomach was growling. I went inside and presented the eggs to my mother, announcing that they were a gift from my grandma to thank her for sending us to help around the house. My mother was pleased, and my sisters were happy too. We opened the melted chocolates and licked the silver wrappers clean.

I thought about what had happened to Rami. I couldn't get it out of my mind. Kifah reported that she'd overheard al-Bilbeisi telling our father that Rami had turned to religion after confessing to killing Nidal, who had been in a relationship with his sister Randa. Nidal had taken her virginity, pressuring her with promises of love and marriage. I didn't know what to believe. I knew Rami had left the Strip before Nidal was killed. But I also had a clear recollection of that rainy night when I saw him, his shirt covered in blood. In our poor neighborhood, when boredom sets in, imaginations run wild. Gossip becomes the currency of the people.

My immediate reaction was that it was a lie. Sure, Rami could fly into fits of rage. He might even fight; he could very well hit or kick someone. But things would never get to the point of actual murder. I didn't believe a word my sister was saying. I knew how much al-Bilbeisi hated the Abu Kirsh family, especially Rami. He'd harassed Rami's mother when she refused to marry him, and Rami attacked his shop in response. My head spun trying to decipher this years-old mystery. I wished I could talk to Abdullah. He'd help me figure out what was happening with his brother.

XII

We were outside hanging laundry on the line with Amal when a plump older woman approached the iron door of our house. She was wearing a dayr, those long black cotton skirts Gazan women layer over their dresses. She peeked at us from behind the blanket we'd hung. Amal was adjusting a white sheet.

"Assalamu alaykum."

"Wa alaykum assalam."

"Where's your mom, habibti? I'm Zahraa Abu Ras al-Barbarawi from the Jabalia camp. I'm just dropping in to say hello to your mother and father."

"Come on in, auntie, you're most welcome."

Amal showed the woman in and hurried to call my mother to come greet her. Then she came back to help us finish hanging out the washing. Kifah took some sardines out behind the house to clean them. Sabreen and I left Amal to deal with the laundry and helped Kifah by pulling the heads off the little fish. We'd grab each one immediately after and throw it to the neighborhood alley cats from atop the wall behind our house.

"Get down here right now, you naughty girls. You two. Now. What are you doing up there? Aren't you embarrassed to be behaving like this? I can't believe you're still climbing up on walls at your age. Get down here."

Sabreen and I went to wash our hands. That's when we bumped into the elderly lady again. Our mother, beaming, was lightly tugging at her guest's arm as she headed toward the door to leave.

"Oh, but it's still early, don't leave yet. Please stay and have lunch with us."

"I'm really sorry, but I'm actually a bit pressed today. I have a few more people to visit before noon, if I can."

"Well then my dear, of course we understand and we appreciate your visit. You're welcome any time."

"Yalla, I'm off then."

"Have a good day!"

My mother went back to the kitchen, a hint of a smile still dancing on her face. She was waiting for my father to return from his friend Saad al-Sarif's place. She washed the sardines, breaded them in flour, and threw them into bubbling hot oil. She then laid them out flat on layers of newspaper to soak up the oil. She arranged the pieces carefully on a brown glass plate, squeezed some lemon juice over them, and sprinkled freshly chopped parsley on top. She heated up some bread and told us to roll out the mat on the floor and put out the plates and dishes so we could eat. Then we all sat down and ate our meal. We set aside some fish for my father in the refrigerator. When he came home, she warmed up his food and brought it to him. She banished us and closed the door so they could talk privately. We went outside behind the house to play.

Just two days later, my mother and father came with us when we went to Grandpa Abu Shanab's house, which was unusual. Normally, my mother just sent us while she and my father stayed home with Grandma Hadbaa to look after my Grandpa Abu Diab, who was sick. They also wanted to be there in case someone dropped by. So we'd go by ourselves and help our other grandma with her housework. We were even more surprised to hear the voice of that same plump older woman when we got there. She was sitting in the front room that my grandpa used to receive guests. She was with a bearded man, his black hair streaked with gray. He was tall, tanned, and wore a red-checkered keffiyeh over his broad shoulders. When we got there, Grandma Amneh rushed over and ushered my mother and that woman into another room where the women were sitting. My father stayed back with Grandpa and that man who nobody knew.

Ordering us to the kitchen to prepare tea, coffee, and fruit for everyone, my grandmother shut the door in our faces. Less than half an hour later, my mother poked her head in and told Amal to come and serve the tea. Kifah and I were to stay behind. We continued cutting up the fruit and putting it in little serving bowls.

Seeing Amal enter the room where all the women were sitting, I knew something was off. My mother never let us sit in the room with the adult women and would scold us if we tried. Luckily, she hadn't shut the door properly, so Kifah and I were able to peep in through the crack, trying to make sense of what was going on. We could see Amal standing in the middle of the room. That woman was circling her, touching her loose, long black hair. Then she inspected her hips. I had no clue what this was all about, but I noticed a smile forming on Kifah's lips. As Amal made a move to leave the room, we fled from our spot by the door. But as soon as she was out, I grabbed her hand.

"What was that? Why did they take you in there? What did that woman want with your hips and your hair?"

"I don't know, but Mom told me to let my hair down so that woman could see it. Then she asked me to spin around so she could see my curves."

"Huh? What do you mean, see your hair and curves? Do you think she's a ghoul like the ones Mom always warns us about?"

"I don't know. Mom and Grandma told me there was nothing to worry about."

I was weirded out by the whole situation with Amal. I asked Kifah what she thought; she told me that Amal was ill, touched by the jinn, and maybe our grandfather had asked this woman to heal her because she was some sort of witch who could use magic to heal people and families. I was inclined to believe Kifah because I'd noticed that Amal was regularly getting strange pains in her belly each month and she'd lost her appetite after she found out about Grandpa Abu Diab's illness. But then Kifah got up and in one breath both announced that she was going to join Amal in the kitchen to help her prepare bowls of nuts for the guests and that I could go play with Sabreen out back.

We all returned to Abu Diab's house that night. We washed up and put on our white cotton nightdresses. We got into bed, but our mother and father stayed up late in the sitting room, Grandma Hadbaa snoozing peacefully beside them. I pretended to go to the bathroom to eavesdrop on their conversation through the corridor wall separating our bedroom from the sitting room.

"She's in love ... I saw her drawing little hearts all over her schoolbooks."

"Come on, woman, there's nothing wrong with her. If this is about her appetite, I'll buy her a pill to bring it back. Problem solved."

"Listen to me, it's like I've been telling you—she's been off ever since she started hanging around with the girls from Qatatwa at school. That's when this all started."

"Calm down. Stop exaggerating. Whatever's written will be."

"Fine then. He's a decent guy, a gentleman. Wouldn't it be better to get this all settled? And it might even open doors for her sisters soon."

"Let's see what happens. Now let me get a couple hours of sleep. They're going to be here early tomorrow."

Grandma Hadbaa's cough startled me. I dashed to the bedroom, where I was supposed to be fast asleep like the rest of my sisters. I was thrown off by what I'd heard my mother say to my father. I felt like she was up to something, something that concerned Amal and that woman. My mother helped Grandma Hadbaa to the bathroom. I closed my eyes and fell asleep next to my sisters.

When we woke the next morning, we had to go back to my Grandpa Abu Shanab's. There were huge trays of knafeh and baklava all around the house. And in the biggest room, there was that woman again, beside the man with the gray-streaked hair. An old man wearing a gray turban was seated next to my grandpa. My mother whisked Amal off to my grandmother's bedroom. They put makeup on her and made her change into a colorful printed dress like the ones we used to wear on Eid in Boumaiz. My grandfather's neighbor Umm al-Abed had lent it to her. She owned a shop that rented out engagement and wedding clothes.

Amal finally went out into the big room. The woman sat her down near the strange man with the red keffiyeh draped over his shoulders. Everyone recited the Fatiha. My mother was overjoyed. She began serving tea and sweets to the guests. Amal then walked out on the veranda where my sisters and I were standing in a line, our backs against the wall. We were monitoring every detail of what was happening inside. And when I saw Kifah's tears, it all became even more alarming. My Grandma Amneh was scolding her. "Settle down … why are you making such a fuss? Are you jealous of your sister, or what?"

The woman started ululating and everyone joined in with zaghareeds. My grandmother's traditional Palestinian wedding chants rang out around the house:

> *Eweee-ha, we came in riding on horses,*
> *Eweee-ha, with silk covering our arms down to our fingertips*
> *… Lululululu!*

Kifah joined us on the veranda, now openly weeping. Seeing her crying, we all started crying too. We didn't understand what was going on. Her voice breaking, she choked out, "Amal … they signed her wedding contract. Grandma Amneh tricked Mom into marrying her off. Amal isn't coming back to the village with us."

I couldn't believe what I was hearing. Amal was so young. She wasn't even fourteen and still had school exams coming up. How could I even believe Kifah? She was the one who'd first told me that this woman was a witch who'd cure Amal of her monthly pains. I scanned the room once again. I saw the strange man leaning over to whisper in Amal's ear. She smiled demurely without looking at him directly. I pushed Kifah away and snatched the knife she was using to cut the fruit right out of her hand. I ran out the front door, right into my grandfather's garden. My mind was racing with everything that was happening, the shock of it. Kifah had lied about Rami, and now Amal too! I could hear the zaghareeds clearly from where I was standing. Kifah was telling the truth, there was no doubt left now. It wasn't Amal's fault that her face was as round as the moon or that she'd inherited Grandma Hadbaa's pale skin. It was a reality here in the African Quarter, named for its Afro-Palestinian residents, descended from slavery, that folks were obsessed with whiteness. Women wanted their sons to marry fairer women so as to produce light-skinned offspring who looked more like Europeans than the people around them.

I could hear the traditional wedding chants and found myself wishing that a wasp would fly right into my grandma's mouth and get stuck in her throat. I pictured how she'd choke and die while trilling because of what she'd done. I started ripping tomatoes off the vine and flinging them against the wall. I dug up the soil, uprooted all the Damask roses. I took out my rage on the roses, knowing that my grandfather had nurtured them with love and care. I even cut off their roots so my grandfather's weak heart would give out over his grief. But I still wanted revenge on my grandmother. I opened the door of the chicken coop and kicked at them so they'd run into the street separating my grandfather's house from the African neighbors. I knew my racist grandmother would die of rage if the neighbors got their eggs for free.

Leaving the door to the house wide open, I ran off. I must have subconsciously led myself to the cactus grove. I opened the gate and went in. I was so enraged that I could hardly see in front of me. I started digging up the sand, searching for Randa's body, which everyone in the neighborhood claimed was buried somewhere around here.

But I found nothing. So I raced to the other end of the grove, indifferent to the cactus needles pricking me all over. I slammed right into a boy cleaning some stones with water. I flailed at him, trying to move him out of my way. I could hear him laughing at me.

"What's up with you, stupid? Why are you hitting me?"

"You're all traitors," I shouted back. "All of you in this damned neighborhood are traitors and spies, you're all working with the occupation!"

The boy had no idea what was going on. He followed me, trying to calm me down. My scarf caught on a cactus. I tried to yank it off and it tore. The boy picked up the torn bit and poked fun at me.

"What? You mean you don't recognize me? You idiot, don't you know who I am?"

"Just another lowlife. What else? There's nothing else around here."

"Alright, take a breath. Calm down so we can actually talk for a minute."

"What do you want from me? Go away or I'll scream."

"I'm Abdullah! Don't you remember me?"

I froze. I turned around and took a longer look at him, paying closer attention to his features. He hadn't changed. He looked the same as ever, only more handsome. He smiled, his same perfect smile. There he was, standing right in front of me, like we'd never left the grove. He was struggling to contain his laughter for fear I might blow up on him again. He kneaded his lips between his fingers trying to conceal a smile. I was so wound up that I didn't know how to act. I tried to speak but words escaped me. My mouth was sewn shut. The person I'd been waiting for was standing right in front of me, in the flesh, making fun of my anger. I don't think I'd ever expected to see him again. But just as I came back to myself, it clicked that he hadn't asked around about me. He hadn't rushed, breathless, to see me, even though he must have known that I was back. I was sure that Rami would have told him. I looked right at him and, in one swift motion, slapped him hard across the face. Then I ran away, back the way I'd come from.

I felt his footsteps speeding behind me to catch up with me. I lifted the hem of my dress, muddied with damp soil, and ran faster. He raced after me, close behind. I ducked in the narrow alleys, crisscrossing between the crowded houses of the Jabalia camp, next to the cactus grove. I snuck a look from behind a wall to make sure he hadn't seen me. I could hear his laughing voice as he walked off: "I love you, crazy."

I stuffed the end of my scarf in my mouth to muffle my sobs. Tears burned my eyes. I toyed with the idea that I'd fantasized the whole thing. I dried my eyes and dabbed at my nose with my sleeve. I couldn't tell if I was laughing or crying. His voice echoed in my ears, "I love you, crazy." I wished that fool had followed me into this alley and hidden with me so I could kiss him on the cheek. I was thrilled to have seen him again after having been suddenly separated for so long, but then Amal's dire situation hit me once again. And it brought me right back to the stench of garbage in the alley, the meowing of hungry cats, and an old man telling off the children whose ball had strayed into his yard.

Spent, I made my way back to Grandpa Abu Diab's house. I found him asleep in his bed. Back pressed against the wall, I sat next to him and lost myself in his wrinkles, the fire he'd kindled for Grandma Hadbaa, the sound of the wood being devoured by the flames. It brought to mind all of the photos and identity documents that my grandmother had burned, unaware at the time that she was burning a past that would never return. Now all we had left were the bedtime stories that kept us up at night, afraid of the ghoul who tried to eat Jbene under the sycamore fig tree.

My eyes rested on my grandmother's shiny silver bracelets and the traditional green tattoos adorning her chin and forehead. I realized at that moment how beautiful she was with her charcoal-gray braids the color of the ash gathered in the copper brazier in front of me. I thought about the story of my grandfather's love and devotion to her, despite men of his tribe often marrying more than one wife. It was so sweet how he tried to help her heal and give her back everything that the occupation had stolen from her. Thoughts of Abdullah seeped into my mind—perhaps he was like my grandfather. He'd kept his feelings for me quiet all this time. But I hadn't forgotten how he used to look out for me from his veranda to keep me safe from Nidal and the Israeli soldiers, all those times my mother would send me out late in the evening to buy something we needed from al-Bilbeisi's shop. I shared my grandfather's pillow, resting my head on a corner. I fell asleep next to the warm brazier, waiting for my parents and sisters to come back from my other grandparents' house.

A loud knock on the door woke me. It was morning. I opened it to find Sabreen asking me to get some more glass cups and coffee pots ready so we could take them to Grandpa Abu Shanab's house. We went in and found it filled with well-wishers. I headed straight to my grandma's bedroom, searching for Amal. Instead, I found the daughter of Umm Abed, the lady who rented out engagement and wedding clothes. She appeared before me like a tight-jeans, crop-top-wearing demon, complete with big red plastic hoop earrings. She slipped a tape into the silver cassette player and turned George Wassouf's voice up loud. She'd styled her hair in large curls with a high wave up-comb, held in place with barrettes and hairspray. Chewing her gum provocatively, she ordered me out of the room.

I stomped out, leaving the door slightly ajar so I could keep tabs on what she was doing to my sister. I clutched the handle tightly so it wouldn't shut by mistake. Even from where I was standing, I could smell the hairspray and hear the annoying sound of the hairdryer and a generator, connected by a long cord from her father Abu Abed's house. I caught a glimpse of Amal's round face in the mirror. The woman was styling her jet-black hair, tying it up with a glittery golden ribbon. She also applied gold-flecked powder to her cheeks and her décolleté. Then she asked Amal to tilt her head back and hold still so she could apply her foundation. Amal smiled timidly when she asked her to part her lips a bit so she could fix her lipstick.

Sabreen and Kifah were crowding me, trying to have a peek themselves at what was happening. They kept pushing me, my grip loosened, and the door swung open. I was rooted to my spot. Angry, the woman rushed over and pushed me away forcefully, "I told you to get out and shut the door. Do I need to call your mother on you? This room is off-limits to children."

She shoved me out so she could close the door. I kicked her foot and dashed to Amal, "Get your filthy hands off my sister, do you hear me? Don't you lay another finger on her!"

She blew a bubble with her chewing gum and popped it right in my face. She sneered at me, "Jealous much? Do you want me to do your makeup like hers? Sit down here on the bed, I'll do you next!"

Her mocking tone sent me into a silent rage. But when I heard my Grandma Amneh's voice getting closer, I sped off. Zaghareeds and wedding songs filled my grandparents' house, drumming and traditional chants filled the streets outside. My father wrapped my sister in the cloak that had belonged to his own father, Harb, who'd refused to attend the wedding. The bride and groom were surrounded by rows of people clapping and dancing as they proceeded from my grandpa's house to the groom's. Once there, everyone gathered on the groom's rooftop, which was two stories up. The newlyweds sat next to each other on a large wooden platform that was set up for the occasion and decorated with a giant red keffiyeh. Pictures of George Habash, Che Guevara, and the groom's brother who was martyred at the beginning of the Intifada hung behind them.

My father sat on a white plastic chair next to the platform to receive well-wishers. My mother danced, fixing her scarf as she and my Grandma Amneh continued singing and trilling. She patted the sweat from her face. It was so humid. Kohl streaked down from her tired, bloodshot eyes. The groom and the other young men danced a traditional Palestinian dabke. I caught sight of Rami and Abdullah's mom congratulating my own mother, and then Abdullah behind her. My mother pinched his ear teasingly as he cast shy glances around, scanning the crowd for me. I quickly turned back to the circle of dancing men, trying to act like I didn't know he was there. I looked up seconds later but he'd already gone. His mom whispered something in my mom's ear. Whatever it was made her smile, and she sang out:

Let the sun set,
And let her not find my lover and me.

It was so embarrassing. I climbed up on a plastic chair to reach the top wall of the roof and looked out over the street to see where he'd gone. I spotted him moving away, disappearing into the neighborhood. The music was getting louder. The girls there were dancing to Hakim's song, "*Ah yani ...*"

It was late at night when everyone started heading home. I went back to Grandpa Abu Diab's house so I could check in on him and my grandma. Only the bride and groom's relatives were left on the roof. Everyone escorted the two of them down to their bedroom. They affixed a branch of henna flowers and basil leaves on the wall with dough. My parents and the groom's parents went back up to the roof together, the night not over for them yet. Kifah and Sabreen chatted with the groom's sisters.

In the morning, my mother and Kifah went to visit Amal and check on how her wedding night had gone. And when a week had gone by, we started packing up. It was time to go back to Boumaiz. The night of the wedding was the last time I'd seen Amal's face. The last time I'd seen Abdullah.

Once we were sure that my grandpa was doing better, we said goodbye to him and Grandma Hadbaa. We crammed ourselves into Saad al-Sarif's car so he could take us to where the border taxis waited. After we'd made it to the Jordanian border, we piled into my father's car. This time, I sat next to Kifah in what used to be Amal's seat. Sabreen stayed in the back. I looked through the window at the starless night. Somehow I could no longer bother to count the massive street lights lining the road. That night, there was no moon. The heavy dark sky served as another reminder of Amal's absence. And I hadn't been able to say goodbye to Abdullah—again. There was no use in crying. All the tears in the world couldn't save me from the pain of being wrenched away from my memories. From my dreams, from feeling any type of joy. I gave in to the darkness. I rested my head against the windowpane. I wanted to sleep. But not to dream.

XIII

Amal had been married five years when my father decided to be rid of me too. The burden of having all those daughters to feed in our little house in Boumaiz weighed heavily on him. I returned with him to Gaza to enroll at the university that Arafat had opened after the Intifada had been put down with the peace process. It was the summer of 1997 and I was eighteen years old. I was so happy to be back in the Strip again, away from the stifling heat that held Boumaiz in its grip. So physically present and oppressive, this heat was no different from my father's viselike grip on my wrist as he dragged me to the print and photo shop close to campus. He needed to make copies of my identity documents and get some photos taken of me to complete my registration file.

He wore his white jellabiya with white cotton pants under it that day, just like the Bedouins in Boumaiz. I was ashamed to be seen with him. Everyone waiting in line outside the shop was staring at us like we were from another planet. I stood beside him waiting our turn. The sun was beating down on us. I wished my father weren't there so I could take off my black hijab, which was weighing on me like the heavy blanket my mother only brought out on the coldest winter nights. Every time I sighed, two angry eyes bored into me and shut me up on the spot. Sweat rolled off our skin, mine and his. It darkened the back of his jellabiya. What made the heat even more unbearable was the long skirt that my mother had made me, in the good luck color of pistachio green for my first day at university. But the scorching heat turned good luck to bad. It felt like we'd brought the infernally hot desert here with us, and on top of everything I was starting to smell. I hoped that no one would notice.

It was finally my turn. My father and I went inside. He spoke to the owner of the shop while I walked over to the little mirror, its blue plastic frame broken at the top, to adjust my long black headscarf. There was an electric fan facing the customers right next to the photography chair. I stood in front of it and leaned my face into the blowing air for some relief. My father watched my every move, even as the shop owner was talking to him, leafing through our identity papers.

"Hajj, are you the son of Abu Diab from the African Quarter?"

"Yes, I am."

"I'm Muhammad Abu Samra. My parents used to be your neighbors."

"Ahlan wa sahlan, it's nice to meet you. Please, can you speed this up for me, get the girl's photo taken? We're in a bit of a hurry."

"Of course, I'm on it. I'll photocopy your documents first, and then I'll take the photo. It won't come out good if she's sweaty. It'll show. She'll come out shiny."

"Alright, go ahead and start with the documents then. Thank you."

"At your service, Hajj. My dad, rest his soul, was always saying good things about your late father, Abu Diab."

"God rest their souls and the souls of all Muslims."

"You can go ahead and sit down on the chair now, sister. Look straight at the camera. Really, you're so lucky that you can go to university. Our loss is their gain."

My father wasn't impressed by this flattery. He thought it wasn't appropriate coming from a young man. I sat down on the stool and adjusted its height with the lever, raising it a little so that my face would be centered in the frame. The young man asked me to smile. I looked at my father for permission. He shot me a serious look that scared any potential smile away. I stared ahead blankly. The young man printed four ID photos and my father tucked them away into a paper folder with the rest of my identity documents. We then walked to the main university building. We entered the hall of this enormous structure. It was packed with students and their parents. My father stopped a man walking by to ask him where the registrar's office was.

He told him it was one floor up. We made our way up-stairs and joined the long queue. It was so crowded that the boys and girls were pressed together tightly against each other, and this aggravated my father even more. The whole situation annoyed him. He latched onto my arm and kept yanking me away from any other body that he believed came too close to mine.

As I felt him getting increasingly tense, I was terrified into immobility, knowing full well that the slightest movement or look could set him off. I knew he'd make a scene in front of everyone. Whenever someone walked into the office without respecting the queue, more and more voices protested and complained, blending with the shouts of the people working there who were ordering those waiting to stay in line. A phone rang non-stop. I was waiting there with girls who didn't cover their hair and had it specially styled for their first day of university. I was jealous. There were other girls who wore tight jeans, attracting the attention of the guys. I was standing there feeling sorry for myself, resenting my life with goats and chickens in a village called Boumaiz and the long pistachio-green cotton skirt that my mother had sewn for me by hand.

When our turn came, I finally exhaled. We'd been in line for an hour and a half. My father hadn't been allowed to smoke and was barely able to keep his cool. I hoped the registrar wouldn't upset him any further. Waiting for him to return, I pressed the button on top of the fan, and it started to turn, allowing me to breathe in a bit of air. He wasn't gone long and came back in carrying a stack of file folders of different colors. He separated them into two color-coded piles on his desk. He sat down, sighed loudly, took a sip of water, and spoke.

"Please come in and sit down, sir. And you too, young lady, have a seat."

"Thanks very much. I'm here today to register my daughter at the university."

The young man looked at me and asked, "What program would you like to enroll in?"

My father cut me off, though I'd already started to reply. "She wants to sign up for the English Teacher Training program. She's fluent in English already. I want her to become a teacher and help out with our household expenses."

Then I interrupted my father. "Could I please ask you for some water? I'm feeling really dry in here."

"Yes, of course, here you go. It's a bit warm, though, as God has blessed us with heat today. Help yourself."

I drank the water and stared absently at the color-coded folders on his desk.

"Hajj, you should know that there's a lot of demand for the English Teacher Training program. I don't know if they'll take any more students."

This was great news for me. I blurted out, "What about English literature?"

As soon as the question left my mouth, my father's frustration blew back in reply.

"English literature? Shut up and don't be stupid. Reading novels won't fill our stomachs." Being mocked in public by my father like that mortified me. It was a whole new level of embarrassment. Eyes riveted to the floor, I replied weakly, "You're right. I'll study whatever you prefer."

My father pleaded with the registrar to do whatever he could to get me into the English Teacher Training program so I could become a teacher in a girls' school, away from men's wandering eyes. He promised my father that he'd put my name on the waiting list and that when the registration period was over, he'd be able to see things more clearly. We finished up with him and left. I trailed behind my father, who was finally smoking his cigarette. We headed over to the cafeteria to buy a Coke and a small bottle of water.

I wished he'd leave so that I could change my major to English literature before it was too late.

XIV

Reassured that I was settled in with Amal and her husband, Karam, my father said goodbye. He left, his mind at ease. Karam and Amal had moved into my Grandfather Abu Diab's house after he passed away so they could look after my grandma. The minute my father left I breathed a sigh of relief. The very next day, I went to the university to switch my major to English literature. If he ever asked me about it later, I'd simply tell him that they hadn't been able to squeeze me into the English Teacher Training program. It was the first time I felt so happy and free in my own neighborhood and the partially liberated Gaza Strip, like many Palestinians after the end of the Intifada when the Oslo Accords were signed. I was just happy to be free from my father's control. His constant surveillance meant he occupied all the mental space I had. I was terrified of him, of the pain of his insults and beatings.

I spent most of my time in the worlds of the women writers whose inspiring stories saved my life.

Their pride and self-assurance infuriated the men around them. I read Virginia Woolf, Charlotte Brontë, Louisa May Alcott. I could feel them surrounding me, infusing my soul with a spark of life that ignited my sense of freedom and lit my path. I knew that I was no longer alone in the world, that fortune had frowned upon many other unhappy women. Cosette saved me. She took me by the hand and introduced me to Victor Hugo, who wrote her into existence. That's where my passion for French literature, especially *Les Misérables*, began. Literature was my refuge, my savior. It opened my eyes. It gave me hope.

A street was what had separated me from this light. I'd been living underground. Like a mole. Not unlike the Afro-Palestinian community in my neighborhood. I spent hours in the library to escape my bleak reality and transport myself to another, more hopeful one, where poets offer bouquets of wild roses to their lovers. I grew jealous of these women and fantasized that these poems had all been written for me, imagining myself in a horse-drawn carriage whisking me far from my neighborhood, far from Boumaiz. But the librarian's firm voice shattered the fantasy. It jolted me back to reality and the library's closing time.

"Come on, let's go. Time to leave, I've been yelling at you for an hour. We are people too—we need to go home and eat our dinner."

I went from seventh heaven to the university cafeteria. I stood in a growing line of students across from the young man frying falafel. I ordered a sandwich. He put two hot falafels inside, with pickles and freshly sliced tomatoes. I sat on the steps outside, waiting for the lecture to begin.

After a day of classes, I made it a point to come back home late to avoid running into Karam. From time to time, I saw him nose deep in a Russian novel, further confirming my mother's claim that communists are atheists supported by Gorbachev. He was the one with a map-shaped mark on his head, proof that he was going to conquer the world with alcohol and adultery. Karam didn't only read Russian literature, he also secretly wrote letters to people held in occupation prisons. He even decorated the bedroom he shared with my sister by hanging the red-checked keffiyeh he wore to their wedding over their rickety wooden bed. I avoided speaking to him because I could never get over the fact that he had stolen my sister from me. He'd married her when she was still a child. It was only after extensive reading that I came to understand that the marriage of a minor child to an older man should be considered rape, especially when the girl is naïve and inexperienced and knows nothing of sex and sexuality.

When I'd finally make it back to my grandfather's house, I'd sit with Grandma Hadbaa and roll her tobacco cigarettes like my grandfather used to. I'd prop her up against my body to help her get to the bathroom. I'd pour water to flush the toilet, cockroaches scurrying over my feet and legs. I swatted at them and killed them with my sandal. I did the same with all the other creepy-crawly insects in there, like the slugs that fed off the damp in the bathroom, which is also where we washed ourselves and our clothes. The tension only grew between me and Karam when I started to notice how extremely stingy he was. He ate lunch outside of the house every day so that he wouldn't have to provide a meal for the rest of us. I also noticed just how much weight Amal had lost since she'd been married to him. As soon as he wasn't in the room, she'd confide in me about how horribly he treated her and the hell she'd been put through in his family's house.

Amal's mother-in-law Zahraa al-Barbarawi was evil to the point that she used to lock the refrigerator door and tuck the key inside her bra to keep my sister from eating. She'd leave her a kilo of sugar, some salt, a bottle of olive oil, and the stale bread left over that her husband hadn't eaten. And Amal never told our parents about her suffering for fear he would divorce her. Before she'd married, my mother warned her to always keep her husband's secrets, never to tell them to anyone. Hearing her say these things filled me with rage. I wanted to murder him, strangle him with his red-checked keffiyeh, burn all his books and letters, rip up his nationalist speeches. Whatever little money my father occasionally sent me, I shared with her. I bought her kafta and chicken, knowing it would cheer her up. It sent me over the edge when I found out that he'd stolen the gold from her dowry and sold it to build himself an apartment over his family's house and rent it out. After that, every time I saw him I spat on the ground. I tried to kick him out of the house. But this made my sister cry. She begged me to stop so that he wouldn't take it out on her and beat her up.

Karam got a job working as a traffic cop with the Palestinian Authority police force. He worked for a full year and a half with no pay under the pretext that the Israelis were withholding the salaries of employees working for Arafat's government. I was left with no other choice but to come home late at night when he'd already retreated into his room. That way I wouldn't run into him and have to yell at him. I couldn't stop replaying Amal's wedding night in my mind—her timid smile as they painted red lipstick on her little mouth. It all came crashing down on me, the misery that comes with living in this neighborhood.

I was kicked out of university only two weeks after the start of classes. I'd thrown my hijab on the ground and stomped on it in front of our professor, who taught courses on Hadith and the Sira of the Prophet Muhammad. He's the same professor who was always lurking around the women-only building, lying in wait to ambush girls who didn't cover their hair. I'd heard one too many stories of girls he'd sexually harassed in his office. He did this when he got them alone, far from the eyes of people passing by on the university campus. It's like they always say in our neighborhood: the longer the beard, the less virtuous the man.

This Hadith professor shouted at me in front of everyone. He wanted to shame me in front of the other girls because my scarf had slipped and revealed some of my hair. "Cover your head, girl!"

I glared back at him, indignant, scrutinizing his scowling features. Looking at him, I could practically see how all the girls scattered the second he set foot in the building.

"Why don't you lower your eyes when you're in here? This is a building for girls to study in. What are you really doing here anyway?"

He marched up to me, brimming with rage, "You don't respect the rules of the university. You show off your hair, you're rude, and you talk back to your professor."

"This university is run by Arafat, and that means the PLO—not Hamas! Who ever said that girls have to wear the hijab in here anyway? Why don't you save it for the PLO girls?"

His face contorted when he saw no fear in my eyes. Then, in front of everyone, he called the university security guard over to force me off campus.

"Don't touch me, you dirty old man. I know where the exit is."

I walked out. The other girls were all gawking at me, following my every step. It was like I'd killed someone, like I was the one who'd committed a crime. I came back the next morning and saw my name written on a board with the comment that I'd been suspended by the University's Public Security Committee. So I left. I walked straight home, trying to decide what to do. I needed to come up with an excuse to justify to my father why I'd been suspended, why I'd shattered his dream that I'd graduate, teach in a girls' school, and help him out with household expenses, paying for my younger sisters' educations.

I headed to the student office run by Arafat's Fatah movement to object to how the Hadith professor had suspended me when I'd exposed him publicly and called him out for sexually harassing female students in his office. I couldn't get a response from them because my name wasn't on their list of enrolled party members. I didn't even bother trying the Hamas Party's student office. Their hostility was guaranteed; it would dictate their decision before I'd even uttered one word. I experienced that familiar feeling of isolation that had clung to me like a shadow my entire life. I'd even felt it at the Dalal al-Mughrabi School for Refugees, where the teachers favored other teachers' daughters. And here it was again, at the university, where if you aren't registered with a party, you won't find support and protection—even if you're in the right.

I reflected upon the truth of my reality as a refugee from the African Quarter, as someone with no party affiliation. I decided to lean into my suspension and find work to support myself until it was reversed. This had to be better than the alternative humiliation in store for me.

None of us understood what was going on—no one in my neighborhood, or the children born in refugee camps who had grown into young adults. Why did we get complacent? Why did we stop throwing stones at the occupying army? We'd simply exchanged the green Israeli patrol jeeps for the blue ones of the Palestinian Authority Police. We traded round tin plate roofs for tower blocks, VW Beetles for BMWs. We residents of the African Quarter couldn't understand what was happening around us. Why instead of it just being al-Jalaa Street separating us from our fellow citizens, do tower blocks now keep us from the very air we need to breathe? Why were they built to asphyxiate us, to block the sun from filtering through to our houses, which were already suffocatingly close together?

I felt a tightening in my chest, a darkness swallow me whole: years of exile, alienation, occupation, and separation from both childhood friends and my first love. And still, no one paid any attention to our neighborhood—not the police, not the bureau chief, not any political party. No one cared about us. No one cared about our poverty, our hunger, or what was happening to us. We could no longer even taste the salt of the sea when we wanted to. It's fenced off. They don't let us through because we don't have enough money to pay the fees to enter the privatized beaches.

All the stones we'd thrown at the Israelis had been in vain. They'd used them to build the tower blocks that smothered our dreams. Everyone's afraid of everyone else now. The windows we'd opened every morning to say hello to our neighbors we now lock shut. And the sounds that peopled the neighborhood and gave it life slowly diminished and died. The streets of the neighborhood became unrecognizable after they were paved, inviting luxury cars to roam them day and night. No one gets a good night's sleep anymore. Even Umm Riyala moved to Khan Yunis, forced out of her home by rising electricity and water bills and the sanitation tax. Her nemesis Abu Samra took her house. It'd been years since we'd had any news of Abdullah and Rami. Only Grandma Hadbaa remained, with her traditional green face tattoos and long gray braids. She was my one remaining hope.

XV

I found work as a correspondent for a Spanish news agency. That's how I met Talal, a photographer for the Associated Press. We shared an office. Like many others in the neighborhood, we started to squabble when new political parties started popping up everywhere, defending the right of return for refugees and calling for the liberation of Jerusalem. Talal joined Fatah. Much more than me, he put hope and effort into the realization of a just peace with the Israelis. He kept trying to persuade me to think of Oslo as the promise of sight for people whose vision had been shrouded in darkness. To convince me to join Fatah like he did. To see the light.

"Arafat'll kick out the occupiers and open the border. You'll see!"

"Arafat is just as effective as UNRWA giving you Panadol—it might cure your headache, but the real problem is that you've got cancer!"

"So what, you're saying Hamas is better?"

"Hamas, Fatah ... six one, half dozen the other."

"Ah, so it turns out you're one of those PFLP people. That explains it!"

"Wrong again, I'm not PFLP. They're always in our business, and that doesn't work for me. I'm not with anyone."

"So, who's left? You're going to join a Zionist party?"

"Are there only two options? Either you join a party or you're a traitor to your people?"

Talal took photographs for the agency and I wrote copy. We shared news and reports every day. I covered the overcrowded living conditions of people in Jabalia, Nuseirat, Bureij, and Khan Yunis refugee camps, how their hardship was produced by the occupation as well as poverty, unemployment, and rising crime rates. I also wrote about prostitution, human trafficking, and how women's poverty was used to exploit them. Talal warned me that what I was doing was dangerous. His phone call woke me.

"Hello?"

"Hi. They're bombing Shuja'iya. Yalla, get here fast!"

"OK. Let me throw something on. I'm coming."

I arrived at the neighborhood where I'd been born, where Sakakini lived in his little house. I remembered what my mother used to say about the unlucky day of my birth and how the sewage burst. I saw Talal up ahead, taking photos of the dead and wounded, and I began recording what was going on. The main street was packed with protesters and ambulances trying to cut through the crowd and get to the wounded. I ducked behind a dumpster so I could more safely observe what was happening and scribble everything down. From there, I could see a young man adjusting the keffiyeh covering his face and then helping the demonstrators break large stones into smaller ones to hurl at the soldiers. A dog howled and then suddenly fell limp not far from the corner where it had been hiding. Its eyes were fixed on me; blood spurted profusely from its neck.

When the same young man took cover right by me, I really started to panic. I screamed. He shut me up, pressing his hand tightly over my mouth, communicating his anger through his eyes. He flung himself into the dumpster to hide. To better hide myself, I crawled under it. All the shops on the street had closed. I spied black military boots approaching the dog and I assumed they were searching for the young man. I turned my head toward the corner of the wall, whimpering in fear, pressing my own hand over my mouth so they wouldn't find me and kill me. The muffled sound of one of them slamming a large rock down stopped the dog's moaning. Once I could feel their footsteps moving away, I shifted just enough to see that the dog's head had been smashed in. I started sobbing convulsively and banging my hands and feet on the bottom of the dumpster to force the young man out. Suddenly, I felt a hand violently grab my shoulder. The same man dragged me toward an abandoned building at the end of the street. Then he disappeared.

I got up behind a wall scarred by bullet holes. Through it, I could spot him moving farther away and vanishing among the bodies of other young men as they all dragged the dumpster into the middle of the street. The street filled up again with protesters carrying a body on their shoulders, chanting revolutionary slogans: "With our blood, with our souls, we'll sacrifice ourselves for you, our martyr; with our blood, with our souls, we'll sacrifice ourselves for you, our Palestine."

I saw them hurtling forward, impervious to the falling missiles. Whenever one of them fell, the others immediately rushed over and dragged them to the safer side of the alley. I saw the same young man from earlier light a Molotov cocktail. One arm raised ready to throw it, he suddenly fell to his knees, clutching at his waist. A soldier had pulled the trigger of his gun and shot him in the abdomen. The protesters hurried over to lift him up onto their shoulders and carry him away from the bombing.

XVI

At noon on Friday, I was in the neighborhood with Amal. We went together to the Agency to collect the food rations that we received regularly from Europe: a sack of flour, a bag of rice, two cans of sardines, and a bag of European powdered milk. We stood in line with other men and women waiting their turn. Walking back home, supplies in hand, we passed worshippers on the way to the mosque. Abdul Basit Abdus Samad's voice wafted over the palm fronds shielding the mourning area set up outside Ayyash's house. His son Yahya, the engineer, had been martyred. The Zionist forces had blown up his car. A spy had booby-trapped the front wheel with his own cousin's help. They claimed that they'd received reports that he'd joined the Islamic Jihad movement in the neighborhood and heard of his skill in making hand grenades and suicide belts. I saw Abu Samra's children sitting there among the rows of people gathered to offer condolences. Hassan Abu Riyala was the one offering small cups of bitter coffee to the mourners.

I carried on walking to the local butcher, Abu Muhammad's shop, to buy a chicken for lunch. People were queuing up to pick out their freshly slaughtered meat. I chose a little red chicken. It reminded me of that crazy chicken in Boumaiz, the one that saved itself from my mother's grasp when she tried to slit its throat, running around in dizzy circles splattering blood all over the cotton bedsheets, pushing my mom to lose it that day, ordering me to follow the bird and catch it, and I chased and chased after that chicken until we both collapsed in the scorching desert sands. Abu Muhammad asked me if he should quarter it for us. I told him that we were going to stuff it, so he just handed it to me. I went back home and gave the chicken to Amal to prepare. I then tuned the radio into BBC-London so we could hear the world news. My sister cleaned the chicken; I peeled potatoes and onions.

"Should we stop by and offer our condolences? He's been dead five months."

"No...?"

"For God's sake, habibti. Stop it, seriously. Everyone dies here, even kids ..."

She was still talking, but I cut her off. "No, you stop it! Not one more word about this."

The anguish of his death ate away at me. I couldn't speak to anyone about the hollow grief that had set in since I'd read that he'd died, when the cleaner had casually left a newspaper open on my desk. I think that was the moment I lost my own will to live.

After lunch, I went to the martyr's cemetery. I pushed open the heavy gate. I looked at the lines of headstones, the names of martyrs and dates of their death carved on one after the other. I recited the Fatiha and prayed for their souls. I spotted a little boy standing near a grave with his sister. Their mother was there too. I turned toward his grave, and there was Rami, holding a green plastic jug that he was using to clean it. I walked up to him and faltered somewhat over my words trying to say hello. I was ashamed that I had not yet gone to offer his family condolences. I stood there next to him. We just stood there, together, staring at his tombstone. At his name engraved right there in the white stone.

I didn't have the courage to face Rami.

"Rami … I … I …"

I tried to find the right words but he cut off all my failed attempts.

"Not a word!"

The anger in his voice silenced me. As usual I was at a loss. I couldn't tell if he was angry at me because I hadn't set foot in their house since he'd died, or if he was angry because he'd lost his brother. I desperately wished he'd just speak to me and break the deathly silence. I wanted his rage to boil over so together we could cry over it all. But once again he walked away, leaving me to face up to my own grief. That was the last time I'd ever see Rami's face. I'd already decided to leave hell, to escape to a better, calmer, greener place.

TRANSLATORS' NOTE
AND ACKNOWLEDGEMENTS

We finished the translation of *A Long Walk from Gaza*
(صورة مفقودة) during the unfolding of a genocide in
Gaza, in the worst circumstances Palestine has ever
faced, even with the Nakba of 1948.

We have no words to write down as a translators' note,
but we did not want to leave this space blank and fail to
mark this point in time. We watched the places mentioned in this book, the houses, businesses, schools,
hospitals, and lives be bombarded and destroyed live on
our phones. As we were working, and writing this note,
people were being martyred every day, in every terrible
way imaginable. Day after day, we and the author of
this book Asmaa Alatawna exchanged voice notes and
texts and calls about the horror.

Our deepest and most sincere acknowledgements and
thanks are extended to Asmaa—for sharing her story

and for keeping on despite everything. And this extends to the brave and steadfast people of Gaza. Their courage pushes us ever-forward.

This book is a deep and nuanced portrait complete with all the beauty and flaws of Gazan society at its center. Today perhaps we would imagine a different book would be written. *A Long Walk from Gaza* now stands as a testament of a Gaza that will never be the same, one that is destroyed. But it is also here to show that the people will resist and will return. It is a document for our future.

Caline Nasrallah and Michelle Hartman,
Tiohtià:ke/ Montreal

ABOUT THE AUTHOR

Born in Gaza in 1978, **Asmaa Alatawna** is a Palestinian Bedouin from the desert of Al Naqb, and a French citizen and resident of Toulouse since 2001. A graduate of English literature from the University of Al Azhar, she then obtained her masters in geopolitics from Sciences Po. While in Gaza, Asmaa worked at the Spanish press agency EFE. Today, she is a member of the Institute for Experimental Arts La Petite board in the cinema domain. Alatawna is known for her involvement in art and gender issues.

ABOUT THE TRANSLATORS

Caline Nasrallah is a literary translator, editor, and researcher with a focus on language as a feminist tool. She has co-translated two novels, *A Long Walk from Gaza* being her third. Her editing and translation work spans fiction and non-fiction. She endeavors to put language at the service of liberation in each of her projects.

Michelle Hartman is a professor of Arabic Literature at McGill University and literary translator of fiction, based in Montreal. She has written extensively on women's writing and the politics of language use and translation and literary solidarities. She is the translator of several works from Arabic, including Radwa Ashour's memoir *The Journey*, Iman Humaydan's novels *Wild Mulberries* and *Other Lives*, Jana Elhassan's IPAF shortlisted novels *The Ninety-Ninth Floor* and *All the Women Inside Me* as well as Alexandra Chreiteh's novels *Always Coca Cola* and *Ali and His Russian Mother*.

Caline and Michelle have published together two other full-length works, *Without* by Yunis Alakhzami and Nawal Baidoun's *Memoirs of a Militant* (Interlink). They also worked together on translations for *What the War Left Behind: Women's Stories of Struggle and Resistance in Lebanon*.